Kremlin-By-The-Sea

Kremlin-By-The-Sea

A novel by

Ben Walker

Kremlin-By-The-Sea

ISBN 978-0-9666145-6-5

Cover design by Rich Allen
www.richallendesign.com

Published in the United States by
Jamin Press
Jacksonville, FL
www.jaminpress.com

Acknowledgments

Thanks to my friends and colleagues Barbara and Bob Pinkerton, Bob Bliss, and David Dowling for their patience in reading over the manuscript and offering their advice and suggestions.

A special thanks to Preston Haskell for his insights into Russian culture and business practices.

To

Alexandra and Alex Biegler

Note: Russian names of two or three syllables are generally stressed on the next to last syllable. Names of four or more syllables are stressed on the third to last syllable.

Thus, Anna Pavlovna Andropova is pronounced AH-na Pav-LOHV-na An-DROH-pa-va.

CHAPTER 1

I still dream about Elena even though we've been divorced now for three years. And this is all the more awkward when I'm sitting in front of her desk watching, listening, noting her every move, whether she put on her makeup today or washed her hair or left the top button of her blouse unbuttoned or whether there was a new wrinkle or two at the corner of her eyes. She just turned forty-five and except for the slowly emerging crow's feet she could pass for twenty-five.

"I don't trust this man," she was saying.

"What man?"

She frowned. "Aren't you listening? No, you never do–your mind is a thousand miles away, as usual. The Russian guy."

"Oh–yes. I was listening. I was just thinking of something else for a moment."

"Of course you were. Now, are you back on Earth Time?"

"Yes. So what about the Russian guy?"

"He wants me to meet him at the Tudor house on the beach. Eleven o'clock."

"But you're suspicious."

"Now you're tuning in. A woman was raped only last week."

"Raped? Oh, you mean what's her name with Coastal Properties. Did the guy have a Russian accent?"

"No. But who knows? He might adopt a different accent every time he calls a Realtor."

"Could be. No, I think they caught him."

"No, that was another guy. A handyman. Can you go?"

"Sure."

"If you bring me a contract I'll give you fifty percent."

"Fifty? I thought it was 75-25."

"He called *me*–not you."

"Okay. Fifty. Doubtful, though. That turkey's been on the market for years."

"You never know. Some people absolutely wallow in bad taste. Like pigs in–"

She hesitated. Never could utter a four-letter word unless she was drunk. Which was rare.

I rose from my chair.

"You look nice today. New shirt?"

"Sort of. A Christmas present, remember?"

She stared carefully at the shirt. "Oh, yes. You're just now wearing it?"

"I've got others still unopened. Bottom drawer."

She sighed. "One at a time–until they fall apart. Typical male." She looked at her watch. "Go. It's a long way down to South Ponte Vedra."

"I'm gone."

On the way down to the house I thought about my dream. It was Elena, all right. We were having a shower together. She asked why I had so little hair on my chest. I told her it was from pumping iron when I was in high school. The emerging muscles push out the hair follicles. This made her laugh. Then she morphed into Jessica, my former student at Ponce De Leon College. Of course there was no shower there. We were in my office–just as it happened. Fully dressed, except for Jessica's blouse, which was conveniently unbuttoned at the top. Only unlike Elena, it wasn't an oversight. It was on purpose. She was saying something about Dostoevsky. About how much she loved *The Brothers Karamazov*. Why couldn't we read that for class instead of writing these stupid essays about capital punishment and abortion? I agreed, but told her the director of composition insisted that freshmen weren't ready for serious literature. She frowned—a beautiful, thoughtful frown like Elena's. Only Jessica had large breasts. Looming, drooping—but not too much, she was only eighteen—breasts. My hand slips down inside her bra. Mrs. Swenson walks in. The dream soon morphs into another.

Mrs. Swenson was very conscientious. She reported the incident to Dr. Pemberton, the president of the college. He was not amused. Neither was Elena. She filed for divorce about the same time that Jessica's parents filed their civil suit.

I pulled into the driveway of the Tudor place. The gates were open. I parked in one of the parking spaces right next to a bright yellow Lamborghini. Even in Ponte Vedra, this was a rare sight. My ten-year-old Jag looked pretty humble by comparison. Got out of the car, looked around. No one in sight, so I figured he was down on the beach. Went up the steps to the large oaken door and opened the lock box.

"Horoshow!"

I turned to the sound and saw a short, powerfully built middle-aged man in Bermuda shorts and an untucked shirt sporting a pattern of palm trees and beach balls. He wore Birkenstock sandals with black socks.

"Outstanding!" he said in the same thick accent. "You are Gavronski?"

"Mr. Malenkovsky?"

"Da. You speak Russian?"

"A little. My great-grandfather was Russian."

"*Great*-grandfather? A long time ago."

"Da. I mean yes. Can we speak English?"

"Of course. We been speaking English. Or did you not notice because of accent?"

"Oh–your accent is fine. And so is your English."

"Thank you. I study at Moscow Highest Technical School.
Mostly engineering, but English, too."

"Well, Mr. Malenkovsky, why don't we–"

"Call me Max. For Maximilianovich."

"Okay...Max. Shall we go in and have a look?"

"That's why I come, no?" He slapped me on the back–rather
hard, I thought–and laughed. We entered the house.

I usually brace myself when showing this house, anticipat-
ing the shock. But Max seemed absolutely enthralled with the
red leather sofas and chairs, as well as the plum baize-covered
walls adorned with paintings of nude women in provocative
poses. There were some Abstract Expressionist paintings as
well, but they looked like they had been done by hyperactive
kindergartners.

"Horoshow!" Max said. "Outstanding!"

We moved across the white marble floors through the living
room and into a rotunda that featured more artwork, notably
two semi-circular rows of nude statues painted rosy pink with
black pubic hair. The oversized French doors with ornate
gold-plated handles offered a fine view of the pool, the ter-
race, and the ocean beyond.

"C'est magnifique!" Max said.

"Oh–you speak French, too?"

"Only a little. How much they want for house?"

I pulled the printout from my briefcase. "Just reduced to
$9.7 million."

"Reduced? From what?"

"From, uh, $9.9 million."

"Is too much. They take $5 million?"

"I don't know. You'll have to make an offer."

Max looked around the room. "The artwork is–how you say–attached?"

I looked at my printout. No one had ever asked about the artwork. "The owner will sell the artwork separately–for one million dollars."

"One million? My grandson could paint these pictures. I offer them $5 million for the house and $100,000 for the paintings."

"What about the rest of it? The furniture, the statues?"

"$100,000."

"So…$5.2 million?"

"That's it."

We went to the kitchen, which was the only room in the house that wasn't enshrouded with either plum baize or red velvet, and sat down at the butcher block table.

"What about the bedrooms?" I said. "Don't you want to see them?"

"How many?"

"Seven."

"Nice?"

"Very nice."

"Write offer."

"Just want to make sure you know what you're getting."

"Write offer."

No nonsense about this man. He knows what he wants. I wrote the offer.

Back at the office, Elena was dubious.

"$5.2 million? They'll be insulted."

"What was the last offer?"

"It was…let's see, it's been two years. I think it was six."

"Then he's in the ballpark."

"They rejected it outright. Didn't even make a counteroffer."

"But that was two years ago. They must be getting anxious."

"Maybe."

"Who is the seller, anyway?"

"Drug dealer. He's in the Federal Witness Protection Program."

"Since when?"

"Since February, I think."

"I'll bet he could use the money."

"No doubt. Okay, I'll present the offer."

"Where? Raiford?"

"I told you, he's in the Witness Protection Program. The Feds need him. I actually have to submit the offer to them."

"And you thought Max was a shady character."

"I couldn't turn down a $10 million listing. Besides, Eduardo is a nice guy. A gentleman."

I sighed and rose from my chair. "Nice guy gentleman drug dealer. You're dating?"

This really pissed her off.

"No, we're not dating...well, we went out to dinner a couple of times, but that was business."

"And you question my judgment."

"You were married at the time. And the girl was under age."

"She was eighteen–almost nineteen."

Elena laughed that superior, condescending laugh that she had perfected over the course of our marriage. "All right. She was legal. But you cheated. I never cheated on you."

"This conversation is not very productive. You sure you don't want me to present the offer? I'd like to meet this Eduardo character."

"I told you–don't you ever listen? The offer has to go to the Feds first for their approval. Besides, we don't know where

Eduardo lives. Maybe Los Angeles. Maybe Ketchum, Idaho. Who knows?"

My relationship with Elena gets testy sometimes. It works better when we stick to business. After all, she bailed me out after I was fired from the college and nobody else would hire me. Still, working for your ex-wife can be a challenge. Not to mention embarrassing. I get sniggers in the locker room at the club from time to time.

It's after tête-à-têtes like this with Elena that I feel a need for sympathy and support.

I decided to call on Charlotte.

CHAPTER 2

Charlotte is a lawyer. In fact, she's *my* lawyer. A friend recommended her services when I got into trouble at the college. When I first walked into her office, I had one of those distracted moments like I have sometimes with Elena.

She is attractive. Not like Elena or Jessica, but attractive nevertheless. The odd thing is that she doesn't seem to be aware of this. All business, though she is soft-spoken and seems to look into your soul when you offer up your grievances. And I had a lot of grievances, both real and imagined, at our first meeting.

Rather tall, Charlotte is. About five-foot eight. Slim, rather flat-chested. But very pretty, even beautiful at certain angles.

"You look worried, Jake."

"I am...sort of."

She rose from her desk—I always seem to be sitting on the wrong side of a woman's desk these days—and came around to where I had retreated to an armchair like a bird in a nest with a broken wing.

She sat down in the chair next to me and put her hand on mine. "Tell me about it."

She missed her calling. She should have been a psychiatrist.

"I just landed a big one."

"A big what?"

"Contract. Or almost a contract. A $10 million sale."

"Ten million! Oceanfront?"

"Yeah. A Russian guy. Looks like he's going to pay cash. So maybe it'll be a little less than ten million."

"That's wonderful! Then why are you so worried?"

"Because he's kind of a shady character. We don't know where his money comes from."

She withdrew her hand and reached over to her desk where she pushed a button. "Stephanie–hold my calls until I get back to you. Thanks." She turned to me. "You say he's Russian?"

"Yeah. That's all we know about him. And he drives a very expensive car."

"I'll call my friend Anna and check him out."

"Anna?"

"Anna Pavlovna Andropova. I met her in Moscow a couple of years ago at a legal conference. She's a lawyer and knows everybody who's anybody in Russia."

"Really?"

"Really. And not only that she's a terrific singer."

"Singer? What–in her spare time?"

"More or less. She won an amateur opera contest and made her professional debut at the Bolshoi Theatre."

"No kidding?"

"No kidding." She turned back to her desk and again pushed the button. "Stephanie–see if you can get Anna Pavlovna on the line. That's right–in Moscow."

Charlotte turned back to me and smiled. "You're looking good today. That a new shirt?"

"One I've had for a while. Found it unopened in a bottom drawer."

"It becomes you. The colors are right."

"Thanks."

I was already feeling more relaxed. But I was never entirely relaxed with Charlotte. It wasn't just her smarts—she could run circles around my cerebrum like a hare around a tortoise—it was her...well, her reserve. I mean really reserved reserve. To put it plainly, Charlotte was a virgin. Thirty-seven years old and a virgin. I think. Can't be sure, but after a few make-out sessions and some serious checks on my wandering hands, not to mention a few comments on her part about her dating history, I came to this conclusion. Phi Beta Kappa in college. Editor of the law review at Yale, and...Sunday school teacher. Never married. Add it all up and it spells V-I-R-G-I-N.

The buzzer went off. Charlotte pushed the button. "Ms. Parker—Ms. Andropova doesn't answer. I had to leave a message. It's 11pm in Moscow."

"Thank you, Stephanie. I forgot about the time difference." She turned to me. "I'm sure I'll hear from her tomorrow. It's Friday. What are we doing tonight?"

"Tonight? I thought we'd go to a movie."

"*Go* to a movie? Why don't you come over to my place for dinner and then we'll watch one on Netflix?"

"Good idea. What time?"

"Sevenish." She looked at her watch. "I've got a deposition in fifteen minutes. Might be late. Just let yourself in."

For a lawyer, Charlotte was rather careless about security. She kept a key under the doormat. I guess the theory was that no self-respecting thief would think to look there.

I drove back to my condo at the beach—Charlotte's office is in Jacksonville—showered and pulled out another shirt from my bottom drawer. While I hesitated—somehow it didn't seem right to be wearing a shirt given to me by one woman while I was courting another—I got a call from Elena.

"The Feds have accepted the offer. I called Mr. Malenkovsky and he says he wants to close Monday. All cash."

"Monday? Can we do it that fast? What about the inspection?"

"Mr. Malenkovsky says he's satisfied with the property 'as is.'"

"And the Feds?"

"They're delighted. And so is Eduardo. Can you be there at four o'clock on Monday?"

"Sure."

I put on the shirt, polished my loafers, and cranked up the car. Stopped at the liquor store and picked up a good bottle of wine. Charlotte's one of the few women I know who prefers a full-bodied red over a spritzy white.

When I got to her house in San Marco–it was really a fixer-upper that she added a huge master bedroom to with all the bells and whistles–I saw that her car wasn't in the carport. I looked under the mat and, sure enough, there was the key. I let myself in, went to the kitchen–another state-of-the-art upgrade, though rather small–and opened the bottle of wine. Pulled a decanter down from a top shelf and poured the wine into it to let it breathe.

I walked around the living room. Some very nice artwork, oil paintings in the Impressionist style, prints and lithographs of famous artists, and photographs of herself with family members when she was a child. A really cute little girl, tall even then. Her dad was a basketball player, later an attorney. Stay-at-home mom. An only child.

Another prominent photograph was of her and some fellow lawyers at a conference of some kind–Moscow. She was in the middle back row, again since she was the tallest, while just in front of her was a pretty blonde. They were the only two women in the group. The blonde had to be Anna Pavlovna.

As I was contemplating this photo, especially the figure of Ms. Andropova, which was somewhat obscured by a bespectacled bald guy sporting a Vandyke, I heard the door open.

"I see you've spotted Anna." Charlotte closed the door behind her amid crunching paper sounds emanating from her grocery bag. "She is pretty, isn't she?"

"I was looking at you. Good photo."

"Ha!" she said, playfully. "A likely story."

She came to the middle of the room and we exchanged a peck on the lips like couples married for years do.

I laughed. "Well, she *is* attractive. The two of you must have had to fight off these Russian vipers. It's a wonder you got anything done."

"They were very nice, very professional. I didn't have any problem with them, but Anna got three proposals of marriage during the conference. Oh! You brought some wine." She was already in the kitchen now unpacking the groceries. "It'll go great with the steak."

"I'll fire up the grill."

"Speaking of Anna, she returned my call after the deposition."

"Really? Does she know anything about Malenkovsky?"

"I'm afraid so."

"Uh, oh."

"It's not as bad as all that." She started pulling utensils from the drawers. "He *is* a shady character, she says, but very rich. Owns a lot of real estate in Moscow along with some oil fields in Southern Russia. Why don't you pour the wine?"

I poured the libations and after the ritual clinking of glasses along with a toast to my superior sales skills, I headed for the backyard. It was still daylight, being the end of summer, and in any case, the steaks didn't take long to cook.

Good meal, good wine, good movie, good...nap. What? Halfway through the movie I glanced at Charlotte–for some reason I didn't cozy up to her on the sofa but sat in a chair–

and she was fast asleep. This was not an unusual phenomenon during our dates. She got up at five a.m. every day to run six miles, arrived at the office at seven, presided over the morning partners' meeting, went to the courthouse to enter pleadings, took depositions in the afternoon, and was usually in bed by nine pm.

After the movie was over I switched off the set, went to the sofa, and sat down beside her. She felt the pressure of my body on the cushions and her eyes slowly opened.

"Oh, I'm sorry. I didn't realize–"

"You've had a long day," I said. "Would you like me to put you to bed?"

She rose and yawned. "Oh–no, I can manage. Why don't you watch the rest of the movie?"

"The movie's over."

"Oh...I'm so tired."

I picked her up as if she were a child. She protested at first, but only half-heartedly, and I took her to the bedroom where I laid her down on the bed.

"I can't sleep in my clothes," she said.

"I'll help you get undressed."

Suddenly she was wide awake, her eyes like saucers. "Oh, no! I mean, that won't be necessary. Would you like to sleep on the sofa?"

I sighed. "No, thanks. I've got to meet Elena early at the office tomorrow. And it's a long drive back to the beach."

"Okay." She was fast asleep as soon as she hit the pillow.

I let myself out and replaced the key under the mat.

CHAPTER 3

The closing on Monday went smoothly, though there was a delay while we waited for Max's bank in Moscow to wire the money to the attorney's office. Outside, in the parking lot, Max climbed into his Lamborghini and rolled down the window.

"Come to house," he said. "I have proposition for you."

"Now?"

"Yes, now. You have other engagement?"

"Uh, no."

"Then come to house. We celebrate."

I wasn't quite sure what 'celebrate' meant to Max. I assumed it would be cracking open a bottle of champagne. I don't like to drink before 6pm, but what the heck–I had just received the biggest commission of my fledgling real estate career.

Max beat me to the house by about ten minutes. As soon as we turned onto A1A, his bright yellow Lamborghini quickly disappeared from sight like a heat-seeking missile homing in on its target. I tried to keep up for a mile or two, but my old clunker starts rattling and shaking like an aging school bus when the needle approaches ninety. Besides, the cops around here have a habit of lurking behind palmetto bushes. Fortunately, I didn't see any cops. And I suppose if there had been any lying in wait, the missile that was Max's Lamborghini would have hardly registered on their radar guns. Or maybe they took off after him only to give up after a mile or so. When I came along at a mere seventy or eighty, they probably thought I was loafing and wasn't worth the trouble.

Max was waiting for me in the driveway. "What take you so long?" He laughed and slapped me on the back. "English cars no good. Slow and fall apart after 100,000 kilometers. No?"

"It *does* spend a lot of time in the shop," I confessed.

Max laughed again and led the way to the front door. A reversal of our first meeting. He took out his newly acquired key and we went in. "Horoshow!" he said, looking around. "We go sit by pool."

There was a kind of Tiki bar poolside, and Max pulled out a bottle of vodka and a couple of shot glasses. "Stolichnaya– just like at home. Mr. Rodriguez got good taste."

I was tempted to say that Eduardo, as Elena called him, had terrible taste, but I didn't want to bite the hand that fed me.

Max put the shot glasses down on the glass top table and poured the vodka. This isn't my idea of social drinking, but I decided that I needed to humor him.

He raised his glass. "To future!"

I raised my glass and reached across the table to clink it with his, but he didn't seem to notice and tossed the vodka down Then he poured another while I took a sip from my glass.

He looked up at me, surprised that I hadn't tossed it down. "Drink! Drink!"

I hesitated but then thought, oh well, one shot won't hurt me. I tossed it down. It was smooth stuff, went down easily.

"Horoshow!" He poured another into my glass. "Now you make toast."

I thought for a moment, then said, "To Russian-American relations. May they be productive and mutually beneficial."

"Good, good!" He tossed his vodka down and I did the same. He poured us both another glass.

If we kept this up I would have to be carried out on a stretcher. I decided to divert his attention. "What is this proposal you were talking about, Max?"

Max, to my surprise, didn't touch his glass. Instead, he looked at me intently. "You are smart young man. Honest. I trust you."

I didn't know how to answer this, so I remained silent.

"In Russia today," he said, "there is much corruption. One does not know who to trust. You, I can trust."

I didn't know what basis he had for this judgment of my character since I had only written up the offer and showed up for the closing, where, like all good Realtors, I mostly kept my mouth shut. But I was game. What was his proposal?

Max leaned back in his chair and gazed wistfully out at the ocean. It was a clear day with only a few cumulus clouds scudding by and a couple of surfers paddling their boards into the waves. "I need men like you."

Was this typical of Russian negotiating? Beating around the bush? Besides, what was it we were negotiating?

"Real estate transactions in Russia complex," he said. "Complex and simple at same time." He turned back to me. "Complex because of bureaucracy, bribes, etcetera; simple because know right people and close fast, not much paperwork." He laughed and rubbed his wrist. "Here, I almost break hand signing so many papers."

I laughed, too, nodding my head. "Yes, we have too much paperwork here. I agree."

He gazed at me intently. "Come to Russia. I make it worth your trouble."

"Russia? What could I do there?"

"Be my partner. We make team."

"A team? What kind of team?"

"Business team. You be my estate agent."

I was tempted to down the third vodka, but I was already feeling tipsy and didn't want to do or say anything rash. "But I don't have a real estate license in Russia."

Max waved this minor obstacle aside. "No problem. I get you one. No test, no nothing. Cost a few rubles."

I leaned back in my chair. "What would I do? I don't know the market there."

"*I* know it. In fact, already have property picked out in St. Petersburg. Nice office building. Great view of Neva River." He waved his hand towards the ocean. "Like this."

"I don't know," I said. "Would it be on a commission basis?"

"Commission, fee, stock–whatever you want."

"Stock?"

"Da. I create company for that property. Could be others, though. You be the CEO."

"CEO? I don't know anything about running a company."

"Not necessary. I take care of details."

This was more than a little suspicious. "Why don't you make yourself president, or CEO, or whatever the chief officer is called?"

"Russia is not like USA. Politics."

"We have plenty of politics here."

"Not like Russia. Here, government not interfere in business. There, nothing happens without approval of top man."

"Top man? You mean Putin?"

"Yes. We disagree. On many things. But Mr. Putin like Americans. Encourage American investment in Russia. He see your name–poof! Deal is done. He see my name–deal is delayed, tied up in court, maybe months, maybe years, maybe forever. What do you say?"

This was not what I expected. I thought maybe he wanted to buy another beach house, or even some commercial property in Ponte Vedra. "I'll have to run it by my broker."

"Broker? Miss McCrory?"

"Right. I'll need her approval."

Max laughed and tossed down his third shot of vodka. "You American men—you let women have too much power. They should stay at home, raise children."

"Well, some do both. But that's the way things are." I stood up, more to avoid that third glass of vodka than to make an excuse to leave. Though I was more than ready to do that. "I'll talk to Elena tomorrow and let you know."

Max rose slowly from his chair. "What is this Miss McCrory like? I only talk to her on telephone once or twice."

"She's quite reasonable. But a stickler for the rules."

"Stickler?"

"She's very keen on proper procedure—and adhering to the law."

"Yes, yes. That as it should be. Well, you tell her that Maximilianovich Malenkovsky is 'stickler,' too. Always honest and keen, as you say, for the law."

"I'll tell her."

I took my leave while Max remained by the pool, where he sat down and poured himself another vodka, staring at the ocean.

CHAPTER 4

Elena was hardly the 'stickler' that I made her out to be. She was ecstatic that Max wanted me to be his exclusive agent in Russia.

"And he'll bring his friends to Ponte Vedra!" she said. "I've got six oceanfront listings–all on the market for at least six months. If his friends are anything like him, all cash, we'll clean out the inventory and attract new ones!"

"It'll be a regular 'Kremlin-by-the-Sea,'" I said.

"Right. Whatever. Do you have a passport?"

"Sure. We went to Mexico together, remember?"

She frowned. "Oh, yes. That dirty little fishing village you dragged me to. I thought that was ten years ago."

"It was only seven. And you didn't think it was so dirty at the time. 'Beautiful beaches,' you said. 'Unspoiled,' 'Charming.'"

"That was before we discovered roaches in our bed."

"One roach. I dispatched him with my shoe but you refused to sleep in it after that. Thus, the trundle bed. Put a crimp in our love-making."

"I don't remember any love-making."

"That's what I mean."

"Never mind. That's history. When can you leave for Moscow?"

"Max has a private jet in St. Augustine. Anytime."

* * * *

We stopped in Dublin to refuel and got a bite to eat. Max stocks his plane with plenty of vodka and blintzes, but nothing really solid. It also gave us a chance to stretch our legs.

We landed at Sheremetyevo Airport and parked among all the other private jets. I was surprised at how many there were. A lot of rich Russians, apparently, since the demise of the Soviet Union. We walked a short distance to an outlying terminal where the border police took a cursory look at my passport, stamped it, and waved me on. They treated Max like a local potentate, laughed at some joke he made in Russian, and waved him through.

A chauffeur met us at the curb. Meanwhile, one of the two pilots who flew the plane carried our luggage–two small suitcases–and tossed them into the open trunk of a stretch Mercedes.

After a quick tour of Moscow, which included the Kremlin, St. Basil's Cathedral and Lenin's Tomb, we got onto a motorway that took us to a turn-off onto a rural highway that led to Max's dacha about fifty kilometers from the city. This 'dacha' was nestled into a grove of trees and looked like a hunting lodge. We parked in the unpaved driveway, kicking up a good deal of dust in the process, while a man in a sort of livery costume came out to greet us. He stood respectfully a few feet away, hands behind his back, while the chauffeur opened the door to the limousine.

The man in the livery greeted Max with a fawning smile and a little bow, his hands remaining behind his back, while Max clapped him on the shoulder so hard I thought the man might collapse. He was probably in his seventies and looked a bit frail.

"Doo-bray-ootra!" Max said. Which I knew from my scant Russian to mean 'Good morning,' or something close to that.

Then, after mentioning his name, which I gathered to be Grigory, Max launched into a spiel that I didn't understand a word of. But he waved his arms around, indicating that he was not pleased with certain maintenance issues with the property. Grigory nodded vigorously as if these problems would be taken care of in short order. I looked around at the beautiful trees—I think they were birch—that formed a sort of protective horseshoe around the dacha.

Grigory stepped aside and we walked up a gravel path to the front porch where there were wicker chairs with gaily-colored calico cushions and sturdy oak tables laden with baskets of fruit. Max picked up a pear and bit into it.

"Horoshow!" he said. He picked another one up and handed it to me. "Try it. Very sweet. Make fine brandy, eh Grigory?"

Grigory nodded his head. Apparently he knew some English.

I bit into the pear. It *was* very sweet.

The house reminded me a little of the Hansel and Gretel stories—gingerbread-ish. Windows inside and out bordered with curly-cue carvings painted in bright colors. The interior was full of heavy but comfortable-looking furniture, with lots of plush cushions like those on the porch. A big stone fireplace dominated the living room with the stuffed head of a very large and fierce-looking animal baring its teeth. At first I thought it was a bear, but it turned out to be a wild boar. Max noticed that I was staring at it.

"Nasty beast," he said. "Shoot once and he crash into car. Shoot twice and he crash into Grigory. Shoot three times and he stagger into woods but not die. Kill my best dog. Shoot four, five times, finally dead. Two hundred fifty kilos."

About this time, a stout, middle-aged woman appeared wearing a dress that looked like it was cut from the same cloth as the cushions. She was actually rather attractive, with high cheekbones and large black eyes. If I had know more about ethnic groups in Russia at this point, I would have guessed that she was a Tatar. In any case, she smiled warmly as Max introduced her as his wife Irina and she extended her hand.

"Za-*dras*-voo-ty," I said, which means 'how do you do,' and made her think I was fluent in Russian, so she fired off a volley of words that went completely over my head.

Max laughed and explained that I knew as much Russian as she did English. To which she replied, to me, "How are you—nice."

The pleasantries out of the way, Max showed me around the house. He apologized for the rusticity, but said it was a very old dacha once owned by a high-ranking member of the Politburo. It was in disrepair, he said, when he bought it, and he fixed it up along with several upgrades, especially to the plumbing and the kitchen. Indeed, the kitchen was equipped with a Viking gas stove and a Thermador refrigerator with a subzero freezer. Granite countertops. Stuff you could find in most upscale homes in America.

There was a billiard room, a bar, and a large paneled office equipped with telephones, computers, copiers, and a fax machine. Upstairs, there were four bedrooms, all paneled from floor to ceiling with beechwood. There was a conspicuous absence of artwork. I wondered about this, considering that Max had raved about the artwork in the Ponte Vedra house and paid a pretty penny for it. But I didn't want to question his taste. I did, however, ask him about the absence of rugs and carpets, noting that only the guest rooms had a single throw rug at the foot of the bed.

"Security," he said.

"Security?"

"I don't like surprises."

"Oh."

Downstairs again, we went out into the backyard where there was some playground equipment. I had seen some children when I was upstairs, and was curious about who they belonged to. Max and Irina were past the age of having young children.

"Deda! Deda!"

A youngster, about six or seven, with tousled blond hair ran up to Max and into his arms. A little girl, also blond, was close behind.

"Deda! Deda!"

Max introduced me to them as Katerina and Ivan. Ivan stared at me with wonder for a few moments, then politely extended his hand. I shook it and fell back on my limited Russian vocabulary. "Za-*dras*-voo-ty!"

Ivan simply stared uncomprehendingly and looked to Max.

"Amerikanski," Max explained.

Ivan and Katerina stepped back. They seem alarmed, but curious.

"Droog," Max said, with a smile.

I didn't know what a 'droog' was, but the word seemed to break the ice. Ivan and Katerina each grabbed one of my hands and began to drag me to the playground equipment while chatting in Russian, much to Max's amusement.

I spent the next half-hour climbing in and out of boxes and barrels and pushing Ivan and Katerina on a swing suspended from a tall birch tree. I guessed they were Max and Irina's grandchildren and Max later confirmed that, saying their parents were in the city at work.

There seemed to be more servants running around than family members. After the children's parents came by to pick them up at the end of the day, Max told me that dinner would be served at 7pm and disappeared into his office. Irina excused herself and went upstairs.

I retired to my bedroom and called Anna Pavlovna on my cell phone. I was concerned about my ability to communicate with her, but as it turned out she spoke fluent English. She was surprised when I told her that I was staying with Max. She said that she didn't know him personally, but that everybody in Russia knew who he was. She suggested that I visit her on Saturday. I accepted her invitation and after showering and changing my clothes, went downstairs. I encountered Max emerging from his office and told him about my conversation with Anna.

"Anna Pavlovna Andropova?" he said. "How you know her?"

"A friend in Jacksonville suggested I call her. They're both lawyers."

"Da, da. Why you need lawyer?"

"I don't. It's just a courtesy call."

Max stared at me for a moment. "Pyotr take you into city Saturday. Tomorrow we go hunting."

"Hunting?"

"Da. Pheasant season. You like hunt?"

I told him I hadn't hunted in years but I did a little with my father when I was a boy. We went into dinner.

Early the next morning we had a big breakfast of eggs, blintzes, fruit and bacon. Irina was not up. Servants scurried around and served us tea. Then I heard barking.

Four or five men were waiting for us in the yard. It was fall now, and everyone had on camouflage jackets and caps to match. Max introduced me to his friends and we headed out to the field.

There was a bit of snow on the ground that had fallen overnight. I hadn't seen snow since I was in college in New England. But the air felt crisp and invigorating.

I have to say I acquitted myself well out in the field. The sixteen-gauge shotgun I borrowed from Max felt like the one I had as a kid and the stock molded to my cheek and shoulder as if it had been custom-fitted. I bagged six pheasants, two more than Max. One of his friends, a crack shot, had ten to his credit.

We retreated to the house around noon and turned the birds over to the cook, who, along with two other servants, began plucking and cleaning them. Then the fun began.

Max put on some music—plenty of of balalaikas—and offered a series of toasts. After each toast, everyone tossed down a tumbler of vodka and things got a little raucous. Max did one of those squat dances where the dancer folds his arms over his chest and kicks out his legs in every direction. His friends joined in, one at a time, as the others clapped.

When it was my turn, I was already fairly drunk and kept falling down. The others roared with laughter. Finally, I managed a couple of respectable kicks, then collapsed on the sofa. The others danced on.

I must have slept for an hour or two, for when I woke up the music had stopped and everyone had disappeared. I made my way—somewhat wobbily—to the door of Max's office and looked in. He must have heard me coming because he turned around in his swivel chair to face me before I had a chance to knock.

"Feel better?" he said.

"A little. I think I'll go upstairs and take a shower."

"Good idea. You be fresh for dinner. My comrades come back with wives. Make good party."

"Party? I'm not sure I'll be up for another party."

Max laughed. "Not so much drinking. A little wine, perhaps. Then billiards. You as good at billiards as shoot gun?"

"I'm not sure. But I'll give it a try."

He laughed again. "Good boy."

I made my way upstairs and took my clothes off to prepare for a shower but stretched out on the bed and fell asleep again.

CHAPTER 5

I never got a chance to show off my skills with a cue stick. I slept right through till the next morning.

At breakfast, Max made a few cracks about my inability to hold my liquor, but suggested that it was only a matter of experience. "Eat more," he said. "Sausage and cheese best antidote."

The mere suggestion of sausage and cheese made me feel ill, but I managed to get some piroshki down. Piroshki are little meat pastries, kind of like pop-tarts.

Max's chauffeur drove me into Moscow to meet Anna Pavlovna. Along the way, I had to ask him to stop so I could get out and puke. So much for the piroshki.

We pulled up to a high-rise apartment building in the center of the city facing the Moskva River. From the outside it looked a little shabby, with paint peeling off the walls and graffiti around the entrance. I thought of some of the inner-city neighborhoods in America. Could this be the way even professional Russians lived?

The hallway was even more depressing, with graffiti on the walls and the faint stench of urine. The elevator worked, though. I went up to the tenth floor, where the hallway was clean and carpeted and found Anna's apartment. '1007.' Nice that the Russians use Arabic numerals these days. I rang the bell, or rather buzzer, and waited. After a few moments I heard footsteps, then the unmistakable sound of a bolt sliding open along with the rattling of a chain. The door opened.

The group photo in Charlotte's living room didn't do justice to Anna Pavlovna. Blond hair cascading loosely over her shoulders, ice-blue eyes beneath long black eyelashes and cheekbones seemingly chiseled from alabaster marble. Slightly gapped front teeth peeked out from full, fleshy lips. A black satin dress cut modestly low in the front, revealing a bit of cleavage.

"Jacob?"

"Jake," I said. "Anna?"

"Anna Pavlovna," she said with a warm smile. "We still use the patronymic in Russia, though it's rather formal. Please come in."

I stepped inside and looked around. It was a very nice, even elegant apartment. Nothing like the outside of the building and the ground floor. "Russian names are rather confusing to Americans."

She laughed. "It becomes even more confusing when a woman marries."

Deflation. "You're married?"

"No. Not now."

Elation. "Well, you certainly have a beautiful apartment."

"Thank you. Shall we sit on the sofa?"

I thought this was an excellent idea. But before I sat down, I gravitated toward the balcony and looked out over the river. St. Basil's Cathedral was off to the right upstream, with the Kremlin to its left. The Kremlin, after all, was the ancient palace of the Czars. Downstream, a vast expanse of greenery, which I supposed to be Gorky Park. Farther off in the distance were church steeples, while just below us were cruise boats plying the river. Hard to reconcile this idyllic scene with the land that my ancestors fled to escape persecution.

"A delightful view, no?" She came by my side and pressed her body ever so slightly against mine.

"Yes. It certainly is. You're very lucky."

"In many ways, yes. Won't you sit down? We have much to talk about."

She led the way to the sofa and we sat. But not so far apart as, say, Charlotte and I usually did.

"Tell me," she said, "how you came to know Maximilianov Malenkovsky."

"Well," I said, a little distracted by the way she crossed her legs and leaned towards me, "I sold him a house in Ponte Vedra. I thought you knew that."

"Of course. But I didn't know that you and Mr. Malenkovsky had become friends."

"We're not friends, exactly. Max wants me to help him buy some property here in Russia."

"But you're not licensed here."

"No, but Max says it doesn't matter. He'll create a corporation and make me the CEO."

"For what purpose?"

I was beginning to feel uncomfortable. I thought Charlotte had filled her in on all this. "Well, I guess he doesn't want certain people to know that he owns so much property."

"Hmm," she said. She uncrossed her legs. "Would you like some tea?"

I said I would and she got up and went to a dining room table covered with a white linen tablecloth. On it was a large silver samovar with steam floating up from the spout and several teacups in their saucers.

"Sugar?"

"Just a pinch."

She poured the tea, put a teaspoon of sugar in her own cup and a pinch in mine. She returned to the sofa and sat down.

"You know," she said, "that Mr. Malenkovsky has been in trouble with the authorities."

"Uh, no, I didn't know that."

She took a sip of her tea and smiled. "Of course *I* have been in trouble with the authorities as well."

"You? Why?"

"Since the collapse of the Soviet Union things in Russia have been much better. And most of that has been due to the efforts of Mr. Putin. However, Mr. Putin does not like to be challenged. Not in any meaningful way, at least."

"And you challenged him?"

"Yes. As a lawyer, I defended some of his critics. He was not amused."

"So he had you arrested?"

"Yes. I, as well as Mr. Malenkovsky, spent some time in the Lubyanka."

I knew about the Lubyanka, but I was too stunned to say anything.

"The Lubyanka prison. Not far from here. In fact, Mr. Malenkovsky and I were there at the same time, but for different reasons. And we never came into contact with each other."

I couldn't imagine anyone, even Mr. Putin, incarcerating this beautiful, poised woman in the most notorious prison in Russia. All I could think of to say was, "How did you get out?"

She took another measured sip of her tea. "Mr. Putin is an opera fan. Or so he says. He gave me a choice—either I could remain in the Lubyanka indefinitely or, if I promised to refrain from practising law and focus on my opera career, he would see to it that I was released."

"So you accepted his proposal?"

"Yes. I've had no trouble since. And he frequently attends

my performances. In fact, my operatic career has taken off since my release."

I contemplated this devil's bargain she made. "Any regrets?"

She put her teacup down on the end table. "Some. But the malcontents I defended prior to my incarceration were scoundrels in any case. I would rather see Mr. Putin running the country than them."

I suddenly felt that I was way out of my depth. These were people that were engaged–or had been engaged, in Anna's case–in power politics at the highest level. I decided to change the subject.

"I would love to hear you sing," I said.

"Now?"

"I mean at the opera house."

"Oh–at the Bolshoi. Well, I will be performing there next Friday night. It's sold out but I could arrange for you to have a ticket."

"That would be terrific. And...perhaps you would like to have dinner afterward."

"Why not? I need to unwind after a performance."

"I could meet you there. Max has given me the use of his limousine. In fact, the chauffeur is waiting outside for me right now. I'd better not keep him too long."

"No, I suppose not."

I put my teacup down on the coffee table and rose to go. She rose, too.

"It's been quite delightful to meet you, Jacob," she said.

"Call me Jake."

"Of course. Charlotte has told me so much about you. You are...dating?"

"Well...sort of. It's more of a business relationship, really. She's done some legal work for me."

"Oh, I see. So you are quite free?"

I wasn't sure whether this was a come-on or not, but couldn't help hoping it was. "Quite free."

We stared into each other's eyes for a moment until I got nervous and extended my hand. "Thank you so much for the tea, Anna Pavlovna. It's been a pleasure to–"

"Oh, you may call me Anna. All my friends do. And I feel already that you are my friend."

"Yes, I feel the same." I was conscious of the fact that I was now holding her hand rather than shaking it. "Yes, well, I'll see you next Friday night. Oh–what time?"

"The curtain goes up at eight o'clock."

"I'll be there."

When I got back to the dacha Max greeted me at the door.

"How is Anna Pavlovna?" he said.

"Fine. And very beautiful. I always thought opera singers were fat."

Max laughed and gave me one of his bear paw slaps on the back. "Not all of them. Come and tell me about your interview. She say anything about me?"

"You? Well, actually she did. She said you were in the Lubyanka together."

"Not together. I never saw her."

"That's what she said. But she didn't explain why you were there."

Max shrugged. "Politics. Mr. Putin does not like competition. Come, the cook has prepared the pheasants. You like a drink?"

"It's a little early for me. I'm still trying to recover from last night."

Max laughed and gave me another hearty slap on the back. "Tonight, I teach you how to drink vodka. Today we drink good Russian cider. Good with pheasant. But first come into my office. We have business to discuss."

CHAPTER 6

The 'business' that Max wanted to discuss was the purchase of a high-rise office building in St. Petersburg. We flew to St. Petersburg in the morning–I managed to get to bed early without consuming vast quantities of vodka–and were there in less than an hour.

St. Petersburg is a beautiful city with all the architectural marvels that Peter the Great's treasury could afford at the time. The Neva River runs through it, but unlike the Moskva, there are numerous canals that branch off of it, like those in Venice. Taking up several city blocks along the river is the Hermitage, or Winter Palace, said to contain the largest collection of paintings in the world.

After a short tour, Max directed the cab driver to an 'estate' office, as they call them in Russia, and an eager young man in a blue serge suit and short black hair escorted us to a high-rise building overlooking the Neva. It was about sixteen stories and looked as if it were fairly new. Lots of glass and a shiny metal skin.

The price was one billion roubles. It sounded like a lot to me, but Max said that with the current exchange rate it was only about 15 million dollars. "A bargain," he said.

Back at the estate office, Max haggled with the agent for twenty or thirty minutes, often raising his voice and throwing his arms into the air. I didn't understand a word of it, but

I gathered he was trying to beat the agent down on the price, complaining about various defects of the building, real or imagined. I was familiar with the process, if not the language.

Apparently, the agent was authorized to negotiate on behalf of the owner. This also happens occasionally in the U.S. Finally, they seemed to agree and the agent produced a contract. Max pointed to me and said something. I could only pick up one word: 'Shef.'

Max indicated that I needed to sign the document as CEO of 'MaxCo,' the corporation he had created in his office the previous day. I asked about the money.

"We go to bank, come back."

"We can do it that fast?"

"Da. No problem."

I stared at the contract. It could have said anything. I hesitated. "What about my commission?"

"No commission. You CEO. You get salary and 20,000 shares."

"Twenty thousand shares? How much is the salary?"

"One hundred thousand roubles per year. A token. But the shares worth millions. Many millions. Please sign."

I looked at Max, then the agent, who stared back at me like a salivating puppy waiting for a scrap of meat from the table. "I think I'd better call my broker."

Max frowned. "Okay. Call broker. What her name? Elena. She know good business deal when she see it."

I pulled out my cell phone and pressed the speed dial button. After several seconds during which I imagined signals bouncing off of cell towers and satellites and finally shooting down to Elena's office in Ponte Vedra, she came on the line.

I explained to her the deal. Or least as much as I understood about it.

"You'll be a figurehead," she said. "And as a corporate officer you won't be personally liable if the property goes south. Just like in the States. And all cash? There's no down side."

"Um, then I should sign it?"

"Sign it. Maybe it's a scam. But if the market caves you'll still get your 100,000 roubles–how much is that anyway?"

"About fifteen hundred dollars."

"Sign it."

"Okay."

I picked up the pen and signed the document while the estate agent grinned approvingly and Max slapped me on the back. He said something to the agent and then turned to me. "Next, we go to bank. Be back in fifteen minutes and close deal." He rose from his chair and shook the agent's hand. I followed suit, with grins all around. Then we went to the bank.

The bank officer led us to the vault, where he spun a couple of dials and opened the heavy steel door. Inside, he pulled out a drawer, offered Max a peek, Max nodded, and he counted out fifteen million U.S. dollars and some change. Max examined each packet before it went into his briefcase. That done, the officer indicated that we should go ahead of him and then closed the door behind us and spun the dials.

"Spas-*see*-ba," he said with a little bow.

Then we walked out to the waiting car and returned to the estate office. The deal was done.

We were back in Moscow for dinner.

This time there were none of Max's cronies around to celebrate. For this, I was thankful since I still had not 'learned' to drink vodka in the Russian way. It was just me, Max, and Irina. Max broke out a bottle of vintage champagne, which was much more compatible with my usual drinking habits.

After a toast to our new partnership, Max broached the subject of Anna Pavlovna. Would I see her again?

"As a matter of fact," I said, "she's invited me to attend her performance Friday night. And I invited her to dinner."

Max raised an eyebrow at this. "The opera? And dinner?" He rubbed his chin thoughtfully. "Why not we join you? I would like to meet this Anna Pavlovna."

Irina said something to Max in Russian. Apparently, she was not keen on the idea.

Max waved her objections away. "Nothing political. I want to see if she is this, this 'super star,' as you Americans say. And we have dinner at Cafe Pushkin after. No?"

I didn't like this idea. I wanted to be alone with Anna. Nevertheless, I could hardly deny my host's request, so I said I'd be delighted if he and Irina would join us.

CHAPTER 7

The ways of the rich and powerful are numerous and often reach into the most obscure corners of everyday life. When we arrived at the box office of the Bolshoi, my ticket, with its assigned seat, was awaiting me. Max had phoned in to purchase his and Irina's tickets, but when he discovered that the seats were far away from mine, which was third row center, he asked the girl at the window to switch his for ones next to mine. At first she refused, saying that these seats were reserved by a very important person. Max scoffed at this and slipped her a five thousand rouble note along with his business card. She made the switch.

Once seated, Max called my attention to a short, balding gentleman entering a box seat near the stage. "Putin," he said. The man was preceded by a woman, who I presumed to be his wife. Two other men in dark suits followed and sat directly behind him.

As soon as the audience became aware of his arrival, applause broke out and Putin stood briefly, acknowledged the applause, and sat down again. The orchestra then struck up the overture to *Eugene Onegin*.

I soon forgot about all of the hullabaloo surrounding Putin once Anna Pavlovna appeared on the stage. She somehow seemed even more stunning than when I met her at her apartment. Of course she had on an elaborate costume, which

enhanced the effect. But her voice was more stunning still.
I'm not a connoisseur of opera, or of vocalists in general, but
her voice seemed so clear, so resonant, so full of genuine emo-
tion. I hardly paid attention to what was going on when she
wasn't on stage, eagerly awaiting her next appearance.

At the end of the performance there was a standing ovation.
Bouquets of flowers were thrown on the stage, as seems to be
the custom with opera. Putin stood briefly, joining in on the
applause, unenthusiastically, I thought, as if he were politely
applauding a fellow politician's speech in the Duma. Then he
left.

As the applause died down, I turned to Max and suggested
that he and Irina accompany me backstage to meet Anna. He
demurred, saying he would rather not bump into Putin, who
he assumed would pay his respects as well. He said he and
Irina would meet us at the restaurant, which was only a few
blocks away.

As it turned out, I was not the only admirer of Anna Pavlovna. The backstage corridor was jammed. It took about
fifteen minutes for me to make my way to her door, which
was clearly marked with her name. There were about six guys
ahead of me, all heaping praise on her and presenting her
with bouquets of flowers and generally fawning over her like
so many yelping puppies eager for attention and perhaps a
treat. I suddenly felt foolish and insignificant. I had forgotten to bring any flowers myself. I considered taking a trip to
the bar and having a drink until the others had left, but as I
turned to do so, a tall steely-eyed guy in a navy blue suit appeared at my side and handed me a note.

"From Miss Andropova," he said, in heavily accented English. Then he disappeared down the crowded corridor.

I unfolded the note: 'Meet me at the mezzanine lounge.
Anna.'

I gathered she saw the hopelessness of getting rid of the legion of admirers in her dressing room anytime soon, and besides, she would need time to get out of her costume and dress. So my idea of heading for the bar for a drink wasn't such a bad one after all. Only if I had left a minute earlier, I would've missed the note and maybe gone to the wrong bar.

The mezzanine lounge was nearly empty when I got there. I ordered a scotch and water and sat down at a nearby table. There was a couple necking in the corner and another, older couple, sitting at a table near me looking rather bored as they sipped on a couple of kirs.

I was about to order another scotch when Anna walked in. She was wearing a nearly floor-length coat of some sort– mink? Ermine? I'm not a good judge of animal fur, but it looked very soft, and very expensive. At first I wasn't sure it was her because she was also wearing sunglasses. I suppose, as in the States, celebrities needed these even at night to move around in public without being mobbed by fans.

She spotted me and sat down at my table. "I thought I'd never get away! Of course I don't want to be rude."

"You've got quite a lot of fans," I said. "Would you like a drink?"

"I think I'll wait until we get to the restaurant. You have a reservation? The Pushkin is–"

"Max has taken care of it."

She pulled down her sunglasses and peered over the top at me like Holly Golightly in *Breakfast at Tiffany's*. "Max?"

"He seems to know everybody. And he can get into the most exclusive places at the last minute."

"Yes, I'm sure. But you are saying that he is having dinner with us? I thought–"

"I hoped we could be alone–but when I told him I was meeting you for dinner...well, he sort of invited himself. And his wife, Irina. I couldn't very well say no."

"I suppose not. Shall we go?"

Max had taken the limo to the restaurant, so I flagged down a passing car–you can do this in Moscow–and the driver, an Uzbek plumber according to Anna, got us there in under two minutes. I handed him a wad of roubles and he seemed happy.

The Cafe Pushkin is an elegant townhouse that belonged to an aristocrat before the Revolution. Baroque architecture with gas lamps, floor-to-ceiling windows, ornate wrought iron balconies, all in a pastel pink with white trim. It looked like the kind of place that I not only would like to eat in, but live in.

It was crowded, though. About twenty or thirty people at the front door waiting to get in with the doorman shaking his head. I figured Max had left word that we were his guests, so I started to push my way through the crowd.

"I don't want to go here," Anna said.

I stopped. "What? It looks great–and Max is expecting us."

"I'm tired. And I don't want to sign autographs. Why don't we go to Turandot?"

"Turandot?"

"Yes–it's just as nice and less crowded. No. Tonight it will be the same as here. Why don't we go to my apartment. Are you very hungry?"

"Not really. I had a fairly big meal at the dacha before the show. But we can't just leave."

"Please. Do you like crêpes? I am very good at making crêpes. Lighter than Russian *blinchiki*."

"Well..."

"Please, Jake. I can't abide crowds. Not tonight."

"Okay. I'll tell Max."

She grabbed me by the arm just as I was about to wade into

the crowd. "No–he won't miss us. There's a taxi waiting at the curb."

She practically dragged me to the cab, but I didn't resist. It was late and I didn't relish the thought of getting into a drinking contest with Max.

We climbed into the taxi and headed for Anna's apartment.

After ascending in the darkened elevator we arrived at her door and she fumbled in her purse for her keys. She opened the door and switched on the light. The apartment was an oasis of luxury and good taste above the sea of debris and graffiti that pervaded the lower floors. She went to the balcony and opened the French doors. There was a nice breeze coming in from the river.

"Pour yourself a drink," she said. "I think I'll change into something more comfortable." She disappeared into the bedroom and closed the door behind her.

I went to a credenza against the wall where there was a butler's tray. The usual vodka, scotch, etc., and several liqueurs. I poured myself a glass of apricot brandy and looked around the apartment. Aside from the abstract paintings–far better than the ones Max purchased in Ponte Vedra–I noticed several photographs. Anna standing with a handsome young man against the railing of a boat in what was obviously New York Harbor with the Manhattan skyline in the background. So that was where she perfected her English with an American accent. I wondered how long she was there. Another was of her in an elaborate costume on stage, though she looked a bit plump–more like one expects of opera singers. Still another was an older black and white photo of a woman who looked like Anna but with a 1950's hairstyle and several men around her in military tunics. One of the men looked short and stout with gray hair and a bushy mustache. He was bowing slightly as if to kiss her hand while the older men looked on admiringly.

While I was contemplating this photograph, Anna returned from the bedroom. She was wearing a floor-length kimono, with floral designs against a blue silk background.

"Oh," she said. "You are interested in the photographs?"
"Yes. Very interesting. What is this one of the woman who looks like you but isn't?"

She laughed. "My mother. She was an opera singer as well. In fact, she encouraged me to follow in her footsteps."

"And the older gentleman?"

"Stalin. He was a great admirer of hers. Why don't you open the champagne? I'll get started on the crêpes."

I swallowed the rest of my brandy and set the glass down. "Okay. Where's the champagne?"

"In the fridge. Right next to the caviar. And the cream cheese."

"Crackers?"

"In the cupboard."

We went into the kitchen and went about our respective tasks. It was a rather small kitchen and we kept bumping into each other.

"Sorry," I said.

Then it was her turn. "Sorry."

At the third bump, we were facing each other. Me with a bottle of champagne in one hand and a container of cream cheese in the other, and her with a mixing bowl that came between us. We both laughed.

"I'm afraid I'm rather clumsy offstage," she said.

"On the contrary," I said. "I think you move with a feline grace on or off the stage."

"Feline?"

"Like a cat."

She smiled and put the bowl down. "Champagne first. You

pour and I'll bring the caviar."

I popped the cork and took the bottle into the living room. After a clatter of dishes, she followed and set the plate down on the coffee table. As she bent over to arrange the crackers around the dish of caviar and cream cheese, her kimono fell open slightly and exposed her breasts. She noticed that I noticed, smiled and closed the gown around her with its sash. Then she returned to the kitchen as if she had forgotten something.

I poured the champagne into a couple of flutes at the credenza and she returned to the living room with two tiny silver spoons and held them up like trophies. "For the caviar," she said with a smile. "It can be messy without them."

We stared at each other for a moment as if this last statement were some coded message.

"Oh," she said. "Music. What would you like to hear?"

"I don't know. You choose."

She went to a large piece of furniture that looked like another credenza, the kind that went out of style years ago in the U.S., and put on a vinyl record. Not surprisingly, it was an operatic piece, from *La Bohème*, I think.

"Is that you?" I said.

"No—I wish it were. Mirella Freni. Doesn't she have a wonderful voice?"

"Yes. Yes, she does." I went over to where she was standing and handed her one of the glasses. "But you have a wonderful voice as well. Perhaps you will be as well known in the West someday as you are here."

"Perhaps."

We both drank.

"Come sit on the sofa," she said.

We sat and I raised my glass.

"To your career," I said feebly. I'm not much good at toasts.

She smiled and lightly tapped her glass against mine. "To art, beauty and...love."

Love? I wondered why she threw that in. We drank and suddenly I felt very awkward. I glanced at the photograph of her and her ex-whatever sightseeing in New York. She was decidedly overweight in that photo. I tried to reconcile that image with the one before me. Slim, or she was a far as I could tell without lifting up the hem of her kimono to see for myself. Which I was tempted to do, but I restrained myself.

"How long were you in New York? I asked.

She glanced at the photo. "Oh, about a year. I taught Russian literature at NYU."

"Literature? You were a professor?"

"That was my official title. But really I was only a lawyer and was hired to teach Russian Constitutional law. They decided to make the most of my talents, I suppose, and asked me to teach literature as well. Or maybe they were short-handed in that department."

"You *do* have many talents. I'm afraid I have only one."

"And what is that?"

"Making a mess of things." I grinned sheepishly.

She laughed. "You're being modest. I understand that you also taught literature before you became an estate agent."

"That's true. But I made a mess of it."

She looked at me curiously. "In what way?"

Now I wondered why I had said what I said. I was making a mess of this. "The college where I was teaching didn't approve of my teaching methods."

"Oh? And what were they?"

I felt a bead of sweat on my brow. "Personal instruction with my students–in my office."

She smiled and took another sip of her champagne. "Was she very pretty?"

"Very."

"And quite aggressive, I should think."

"Well...I wouldn't say 'aggressive.' But she was quite eager to, uh, learn."

She seemed to find this quite amusing. "I can understand her...enthusiasm. You are a very attractive man. And of course as a teacher, you are always on stage, a performer like me. Did she sit close to you?"

"In my office?"

"In class."

"She *did* sit in the front row, come to think of it."

"And each day she observed your every movement, the cut of your clothes, the way you gestured to make a point–yes, I can quite understand her 'enthusiasm.'

I looked down at the carpet. "I didn't mean to drag up one of the more sordid incidents of my past. Please forgive me."

"There's nothing to apologize for. I admire your honesty. And there is nothing 'sordid' about giving in to a natural impulse–especially when the other party shares that same impulse. As long as it's discreet, of course."

"Yes. Well, it was discreet until my secretary walked in. I thought the door was locked."

Anna laughed. "You took all necessary precautions–or at least you thought you did. Come–sit closer. You and I have more in common than one might suppose."

I moved closer.

She patted me on the knee. "That's better. I don't like to have to raise my voice. Singing is hard on the vocal cords. Caviar?"

"Sure."

She leaned over and spread some cream cheese on a cracker. Again, the loose gown exposed her breasts. She dished up some caviar with one of the tiny spoons and put it on the cracker. Then she brought it to my mouth. I took a bite, the cracker crumbled, leaving half of it in her hand as she moved quickly to catch the crumbs with her other hand.

She laughed. "You should take it all in one bite."

"Sorry. Not aggressive enough, eh?"

"I should say not. Now–I'll show you." She picked up another cracker, spread the cream cheese on it, topped it with caviar, and gulped it down in one bite. "You see?"

"Yes." She served up another cracker.

I gulped it down. "That's very good caviar."

"Of course. The best in the world."

We both chased the crackers and caviar down with champagne. Then she surprised me. She threw her glass against the fireplace and smashed it to pieces.

I looked at her for a moment, hesitated, then followed suit.

"You are learning the Russian way," she said.

"Seems like a waste of very nice glassware," I said.

"I have more. Are you ready for the crêpes?"

"Ravenous."

She smiled that enigmatic smile of hers, then rose and went into the kitchen.

"Can I help?" I said.

"No. It'll only take a minute."

I began pacing around the living room and finally went to the credenza. "More champagne?"

"Please," she called from the kitchen.

I poured two more glasses. I was beginning to feel a bit tipsy. Or rather euphoric. That was it, really. It wasn't just the alcohol, it was the atmosphere, the music, and especially the proximity of this woman. Her talk of aggression seemed to put my motor into gear. I wondered how she would react if I...

I walked into the kitchen with the glasses in my hand.

"I told you not to come into the kitchen," she said.

"I'm not hungry anymore."

"No?"

"No. Why don't we finish the champagne first?"

"Well...all right."

I handed her a glass. She smiled at me, her long lashes fluttering, a little nervously, I thought. We drank down the champagne.

She put down her glass and leaned against the counter, which was of a cool marble.

I put down my glass. I was standing very close to her now. She seemed amused, as if wondering what I would do.

I leaned forward and kissed her. She seemed agreeable. More than agreeable. She began unbuckling my belt.

I saw this as a very positive development.

She unzipped my pants and reached inside. This was *very* positive. I lifted the hem of her gown to her thighs, but it snagged on the edge of the counter. She pulled away from the counter, withdrew her hand from my shorts, and with an impish smile, loosened the sash and shimmied out of her kimono. She was completely naked now.

I tried to duplicate her shimmy in order to drop my pants to the floor but they only went as far as my knees. She laughed and reached down to help. I felt that we should move to the bedroom, but I was afraid something would be lost in the process. I was ready; she was ready. So I lifted her up onto the counter, her buttocks supporting her weight. Then a thrust upward, rising on my toes.

This seemed to work. I was just tall enough to drive deep inside her, and she was positioned in such a way that her body could accommodate the intrusion.

Not that she considered it an intrusion. At least not an unwelcome one.

CHAPTER 8

Anna and I didn't get around to the crêpes until the next morning. We had breakfast on her little balcony overlooking the river. She asked how long I would remain in Moscow.

"I don't know yet. Max seems to want me to stick around and help him with some real estate purchases."

She shook her head and put her cup of coffee down in its saucer. "It's not good for you to get mixed up with this Malenkovsky man. He has a long history of questionable business practices."

"Questionable? And that's why he was in the Lubyanka?"

"Yes. Although nothing was proven. He was released, as I was, after coming to an agreement with Mr. Putin."

I had the uneasy feeling that Anna was drawing me back into that other world of hers, the world of dark plots and political intrigue. "What kind of agreement?"

She leaned back in her chair. She was wearing that same kimono of the night before, only tightly cinched at the waist. I could see her nipples, though, poking through the thin blue silk. This was distracting, to say the least. "I am not familiar with the details, but I suspect that it was something like you Americans call a 'non-compete' agreement. That is, Mr. Malenkovsky promised not to compete with Mr. Putin in certain areas of business."

I tried to take my eyes off of her lithe figure–an opera singer!–and followed her gaze out over the river. "What areas of business?"

"Oil. Since the collapse of the Soviet Union there has been a movement towards privatisation. There is much competition for the spoils, one might say, in this sector."

"And Mr. Putin wants the lion's share."

"Exactly. They both do."

I considered this. I had already dipped my toe into Max's business pool, and so far, it felt good. I, and Elena, stood to make quite a bit of money from the property in St. Petersburg. But oil! That's where the real money was. On the other hand, maybe we should not be too greedy. Go home, sell the shares, and be content.

"I don't know anything about the oil business."

"Good. Best you go home and forget about Mr. Malenkovsky."

I was a little offended that she suggested that I go home. Did last night mean nothing to her? I decided to test her. "Why don't you come with me?"

She turned away from the river and looked at me with surprise. "With you? To America?"

"That's where I live."

"Of course. But you see...I have a career here."

"You said yourself that you'd like to be better known in the West."

"I didn't say that–you did."

"All right. But wouldn't you?"

She seemed to think about this for a moment. "Yes. I suppose so. But I'd have to go to New York–not Florida."

"New York's only two hours from Florida."

"Yes. But contacts would be difficult to make–and cultivate. That's very important in the world of opera."

"Just a thought. The real reason I'd want you to come is to be with me."

She smiled, more relaxed now. "I should like to come to visit you. Perhaps I could perform in some local productions. For fun, not professionally."

"We could have a great deal of fun."

She smiled again with that 'come hither' smile and I was tempted to carry her back into the bedroom. But she squelched this impulse.

"Mr. Malenkovsky must be wondering where you are."

"I suppose so." I put my napkin down. "I'd better return to the dacha. Can I call you later?"

"Of course."

Anna called Yandex for me, the Russian equivalent to Uber, and by the time I got down to the street the driver was waiting for me.

When I arrived at the dacha, Max came out on the porch with a steaming cup of coffee in his hand, wearing a colorful terry cloth bathrobe. His hair was wet and slicked back as if he had just stepped out of the shower. A big grin on his face.

"I see you take opportunity to know Anna Pavlovna better."

"Yes. Well, she said she wanted to avoid the crowd. We went back to her place. Sorry to stand you up."

"Stand up?"

"Break the date. Not show up."

Max laughed and slapped me on the back. "Not a problem. We have good dinner and go dancing after. But you have own party. Hungry?"

"No thanks. Just had breakfast."

"Come sit with me in office. I have interesting proposition for you. Coffee?"

"Sure." After what Anna told me, I was a little wary now of

Max's propositions. But I followed him into his office where a servant brought a tray with a pot of coffee on it.

Once seated, Max poured himself another cup and leaned back in his chair. I suppose he was a bit hungover, but if so, he showed no signs of it beyond the need for large amounts of coffee.

"You are familiar with Azerbaijan?"

"Azerbaijan? I've heard of it, but I don't know where it is."

"South of Moscow–eighteen hundred kilometers. On the Caspian Sea."

"The Caspian? Yes–I think I know where that is."

"Baku is capital. Very interesting city."

"What's interesting about it?"

"Oil. And the culture. You like to go?"

I thought about my conversation with Anna earlier that morning. The word 'oil' made me uncomfortable. "I think I'd better start thinking about returning to the U.S. I have listings there–clients. They don't like to be neglected."

"Miss McCrory can accommodate them, I'm sure."

This was true. But I couldn't think of a better excuse. "She's very busy herself. I think–"

"Besides, what is commission on this little house, or that little house? One thousand, two thousand dollars?"

"A little more. Usually."

Max drained his cup and poured another. "You want more coffee?"

"I'm okay."

He put down the pot. "In Azerbaijan you can be–how you say in English?–oil baron. Like J.R."

"J.R.?"

"You not watch *Dallas*? Very popular TV show in Russia."

"Oh–that J.R."

"Yes. That J.R. Oil fields in Azerbaijan–just offshore–very

rich. Millions of barrels of proven reserves. I like to show you."

I considered this. "What would be my role?"

"Same as in St. Petersburg. CEO."

I squirmed in my seat. "But at least I know something about real estate. I know nothing about the oil business."

"Not necessary. Is simple. Drill. Pump. Sell."

"Somebody has to do all that."

"Da. Engineers, 'roughnecks,' like you call them in America, salespeople. They work for me. I work for you. Simple."

"Would I have to live here?"

"No. Go home. Sell oceanfront houses to my friends in Moscow. I send you quarterly reports."

I squirmed a little more in my chair. "I would have to sign some papers, of course."

"Of course."

"Well...um, when can we leave?"

"Today. Now."

"Can I take a shower?"

Max laughed and rose from his desk. "Take *two* showers. Americans must be cleanest people in world!"

I managed a little laugh and rose myself. An hour later we were on our way to Baku.

CHAPTER 9

It only took a couple of hours. The pilot circled the city and dipped his wings so I could get a good look at the skyline. It looked like many European cities from the air, though I noticed several minarets erupting from buildings within the walls of the city. Beyond the walls were a group of modern skyscrapers that looked like giant silver flames flickering in the sunlight.

We skirted Aliyev International Airport and landed at Kala airbase, a military base. I asked Max why we were landing there.

"Passports, visas. A nuisance. Besides, they take care of my airplane."

An officer of some kind—couldn't be sure of the rank—met us on the tarmac and after greeting Max with a hearty handshake and politely shaking mine, ushered us into a limousine with a couple of flags mounted on each fender. One was the Russian tricolor—white stripe on top followed by a blue one, then a red one—and the other the Azerbaijani flag with the same horizontal stripes, but blue, red, and green with a crescent moon in the middle about to swallow a white star. These flags drew attention as they fluttered in the breeze and we wound our way through the narrow streets of the old city. Finally we arrived at our destination, the Four Seasons Hotel Baku. This five-star establishment combined old world elegance with new world amenities. Max had rented a suite on the top floor with a balcony that wrapped around the living room for a 180 degree view of the Caspian.

I was beginning to feel like an oil baron already.

After lunch, Max had the desk clerk summon a cab for us–a London-style taxi–and we headed for the harbor. Here we boarded his yacht, a sleek hundred-footer, and took a cruise to inspect the oil fields. I say 'fields,' but they were all under water. The only evidence that they were there was a number of derricks just a few miles offshore that seemed to be in per-petual motion.

"It looks like these fields are already taken," I said, raising my voice over the noise of the engines and the steady breeze.

Max pointed to the featureless landscape to our portside. "You see that?"

I squinted at the land mass. "What? Those brown hills?"

"Da. All land from Baku to Kilyazi belong to my grandfa-ther long time ago. He was Azeri."

"Azeri? You're Azerbaijani?"

"On mother's side. When Revolution come Soviets national-ize oil fields. Grandfather Ali have no political connections and so lose everything–he become common laborer on land he once own."

We both stared at the shoreline in silence for a few mo-ments. Then Max suddenly grabbed at the air as if capturing a fly in mid-flight. "I get it back!"

I stared at him now. "You bought the land back?"

"Da. With help of *my* political connections. You see der-ricks?"

I turned my attention to the shore again. Now I could see the derricks, which were just poking up above the horizon. "I see them."

"Produce maybe 200,000 barrels per day, but offshore fields

capable of 800,000 per day. These fields–" he pointed towards the water "–are future! I show you."

We ventured a little farther out and the captain cut the engines. It was quiet. Max ordered a couple of drinks and we sat on the rear deck at a table. While we were waiting, Max unfurled a map of the seabed. He pointed out the new fields he was interested in. In the distance I noticed a vessel of some kind approaching us. Max looked up.

"A gunboat. Probably Turkmen."

"Turkmen?"

"They claim they own one-fifth of seabed. Exact boundaries in dispute."

The gunboat was rapidly approaching.

"Excuse me," Max said. He rolled up the map and scurried up the ladder to the wheelhouse. I was left standing on the deck with a couple of sailors who seemed nervous. I wondered if we were about to be attacked.

Max descended the ladder and returned to the deck.

"What do they want?" I said.

"To show they control area. We are in Azerbaijani sector. They know that, but wish to impose their will on us. We must humor them."

The gunboat came alongside of us and a couple of uniformed sailors with AK-47s across their chests stood menacingly at either side of a gangplank which was extended to our vessel. In the meantime, a booming voice blared from the gunboat's loudspeaker.

"What's he saying?"

"He wants to come aboard."

"Should we let him?"

Max shrugged his shoulders. "What choice do we have? You see the guns." He signaled the captain, who said something over his loudspeaker. "If we flatter him with his importance, he will soon go away."

Suddenly a man in an officer's uniform appeared at a door to the gunboat's wheelhouse. He mounted the gangplank and came aboard.

He saluted Max, who nodded and said something in Russian. The Turkmen looked around the yacht and brought his eyes back to Max's, then to me. He said something again in Russian. I looked at him blankly.

"Amerikanski," Max said. "Droog."

The Turkmen officer smiled and nodded his head. "Amerikanski. Welcome."

This seemed to break the ice. Suddenly there were smiles all around. The officer said something else to Max in Russian, Max answered, and the officer returned to his gunboat.

After they were gone, I turned to Max. "What was that all about?"

"I told him you were my American guest. In fact, that you are the American Ambassador to Azerbaijan. Congratulations!"

We both laughed and returned to the table where Max unfurled the map again.

Back at the hotel Max suggested we go to the bar to see what women might like to join us for dinner. I refrained from reminding him that he was a married man and said that I needed to call Elena.

"Why you always need to call Elena? You can't make decisions yourself?"

"It's not just business," I said. "I need to find out how the children are doing."

"Children? You have children?"

"Stepchildren. Actually, they're Elena's children from a previous marriage."

"Previous? She is your ex-wife?"

"Exactly."

Max seemed dumbfounded. "You work for your ex-wife?"

"I'm an independent contractor. But, yes, in a way I work for her."

He shook his head. "You American men. Your women dominate you."

"Well, I wouldn't say that, exactly. We're just on a more equal footing these days."

Max was unconvinced. "Equal? You go call Elena. I go see if I can find some 'equal' women in bar. Maybe they pay for drinks." He stalked off towards the bar.

I returned to the room, sat out on the balcony and called Elena on my cell phone. It was early in Ponte Vedra and she was in her office.

"How are the boys?" I said, feeling that I would not have lied to Max if I actually asked about them.

"The boys? They're fine. Where are you?"

"Baku."

"Baku?"

"Azerbaijan. On the beautiful Caspian Sea."

"What are you doing there?"

"Looking at oil fields. That's what I wanted to talk to you about."

I explained the oil deal that Max was trying to put together. "Do you think I ought to sign up for it?"

There was a silence at her end for several seconds. "I don't know. This is out of my bailiwick. And yours, too. Why does he need you?"

"For the same reason that he needed me for the deal in St. Petersburg. He wants to keep a low profile. And he doesn't want to draw the attention of Putin."

"Putin? What does he have to do with Putin?"

"It's complicated. But it seems that Putin is interested in

these same oil fields and as Anna says, he doesn't like competition."

"I don't know, Jake. This all sounds very shaky. You could get into
trouble. *We* could get into trouble. Why don't you call Charlotte? If
she thinks it's legal and aboveboard, go ahead. How much are these
oil fields worth?"

"Billions. As in dollars."

Another long silence. "Oil fields are real estate, aren't they?"

"I suppose so. Even though they're underwater."

"You're my subcontractor."

"Correct."

"If it all works out–"

"Don't worry. I'll give you a cut. The usual sixty-forty."

"You're an angel."

It had been a long time since she had called me that. "I'll keep you
updated."

I hung up and called Charlotte. I explained the deal to her.

"The tax considerations are complex" she said. "And even American law is vague when it comes to 'straw man' deals. I'll need to do
some research."

"What do I do in the meantime?"

"Stall him. Better yet, come home so we can sit down together and
talk about it."

"Why don't you just call Anna? She knows Russian law."

"But does she know Azerbaijani law? Of course I'll call her. But this
could take time. If you stay, Mr. Malenkovsky will put pressure on
you to sign. And there's no other reason for you to be there."

I sighed. I was hoping we could wrap it up. Then I could come
home. "What if *I* call Anna?"

"Sure. Why not? But I have a feeling that she'll give you the same
advice. Don't jump into this."

I hung up the phone and called Anna. No answer. I left a message.

CHAPTER 10

Max brought a couple of 'ladies' up from the bar. I had fallen asleep on the chaise longue on the balcony and one of them woke me up at Max's bidding.

I blinked. She was bronze-skinned with a coil of black hair—a chignon—draped over her shoulder. She had dark eyes and a somewhat upturned nose like a teenage girl who hadn't quite grown up yet. She had a drink in her hand—one of those pink and orange concoctions of various fruit juices mixed with several ounces of vodka. She giggled and said something to me in an unfamiliar language.

"She understands some Russian," Max said, his arm around the waist of the other girl, who had a similar complexion. "She and her friend here are Uzbeks. A barbaric people. But quite charming, don't you think?"

Max put on some music and began dancing with the girl. The other one pulled me to my feet and encouraged me to dance with her, though she apparently got bored with my rather clumsy moves and started dancing with her friend. Max enjoyed their synchronized movements so much that he sat down on the divan with me and began clapping to the tune of the music.

"I think they are sisters," he said. Indeed, they did look alike. At the end of the recording, Max went to the bar and poured everyone a drink. This time some kind of liqueur. He offered a toast in Russian which I didn't understand, but I think it had to do with their dancing skills. They giggled and everyone drank from their glasses.

Max turned to me. "You hungry?" Without waiting for an answer he said, "We go to nice little restaurant I know." He didn't ask the girls if they wanted to go, but simply motioned for them to follow. And they did.

The restaurant looked like an ancient caravansary and might have been one at some point. A cobblestone courtyard with a fountain in the center that led to the main dining room. There were smaller, private rooms that radiated from this. As in Moscow, Max seemed to know the owner and he ushered us into one of the private rooms. There were musicians in the main room, but they wandered around and would often pop into the private rooms unannounced. The food was excellent, mostly consisting of rice and 'dolma' or vegetables stuffed with lamb and sauces seasoned with garlic and other spices. The girls danced again for us and afterwards Max pulled one of them onto his lap. The other came to sit on mine, but I was still eating at the time and gently pushed her away. She seemed offended and went over to Max, who made some remark in Russian, which I gathered alluded to my alleged prudery. Then he started kissing both girls alternately; and they giggled and caressed his chest and belly. I suddenly felt like a fifth wheel and excused myself, saying I didn't feel well, and headed back to the hotel.

I wandered through the streets for a while thinking of Anna. Why hadn't she returned my call? It wasn't so much the oil deal I wanted to discuss with her as just hearing the sound of her voice. She was a fascinating woman, with a mix of intellect and sensuality that I had rarely encountered. Elena certainly wasn't stupid, or lacking in sensuality, but she really didn't share my interests in language and literature. And Charlotte? All brains and ambition. Little time or space left over for 'amour.'

As I ruminated over the women in my life, I suddenly realized I was lost. The ancient streets seemed empty. And dark. I backtracked a little towards the last major street that was well-lit. Then something hit me in the back of the head. At first I thought it was a falling rock, or brick, from one of the buildings. Then a hand grabbed my shoulder and spun me around. I just managed to duck as this shadowy character swung a club of some kind at my head. Out of the corner of my eye I saw another figure, small and lithe, dancing around me as if looking for an opening to attack. I punched the first guy in the face and he seemed shocked for a moment, as if I weren't playing fair. The other one, the little dancer, came at me with a sap of his own and caught me on the side of the head. I went down and that was the last thing I remembered until I woke up several minutes later.

I staggered to my feet and felt my throbbing temple. There was a little blood trickling down my neck and inside my collar, but not much. I checked my pockets. Of course my wallet was gone. And so was my passport. They didn't take my cell phone, however. It was a small one that I kept in my pants pocket rather than my coat pocket.

I called Max, who was still at the restaurant and told him what happened. He apparently was enjoying himself with the girls and told me to continue to the hotel. We would call the police and the U.S. Embassy in the morning and see what we could do about the passport.

When I got back to the hotel I got a call from Anna.

"What are you doing in Baku?" she said.

"Max. He wants to invest in some oil fields."

There was a long silence. "Anna?"

"Yes, I'm here. Why did he take you with him?"

"Well, it's complicated, but it seems he wants to avoid any publicity, so the deal will be in my name. In fact, that's why I called you earlier. I need your advice."

"Don't sign anything. It's sure to come to Mr. Putin's attention. And then you could be in real trouble."

This was a sobering thought. I remembered now Anna's warning about getting mixed up with Max and Putin as they competed with each other.

"Okay," I said. "I won't sign anything until I know more. After I get my passport back, or a duplicate, I'll return to Moscow. I'll call you"

"Passport? What happened to your passport?"

I told her about the robbery.

"Are you hurt?"

"Not really."

"Good. You have called the police?"

"Not yet. Max says to wait till morning and he'll go with me to the police station. I don't speak Azerbaijani—or even Russian, for that matter."

"Hmm. Well, call me when you are through with them. I'm concerned about your safety."

"You are?"

"Of course."

The next morning I managed to rouse Max from his deep slumber and get some coffee into him. He seemed exhausted.

"This fellow hit you with brick?"

"I think it was a blackjack. I'm not sure."

"Blackjack?"

"A club—sort of."

"You need doctor?"

"No. I'll be all right."

As Max was getting dressed, we got a call on the hotel

phone from the police. Max picked up the receiver and listened for a few moments.

"Da. Horoshow." He hung up the receiver and turned to me. "They have your wallet. Passport. Everything."

"Really? How did they–"

"Fellow that hit you with brick try to get on plane to Moscow. Chechen. Want to blow up airplane."

"Blow it up? Good grief!"

"Da. Much grief if he succeed. We go down to station. Identify him."

We went down to the station and sure enough it was one of the guys who jumped me. The little one, the dancer. He claimed he was alone, but I told the cops about his friend and they put out a call to search for him. After signing a form written in Azerbaijani–I had no idea what it said–they gave me my wallet and passport and told me I could go. Even the credit cards were there–the guy had used one to buy his plane ticket.

But just as we were about to leave the man in charge, a captain, put his hand on Max's shoulder. He said something to Max in Russian and Max objected, but the captain nodded to two gentlemen in the corner who we hadn't noticed. They wore plain suits.

Max turned white. The two men in suits came over to him and indicated a room near where they had been standing. Max turned to me.

"Go back to hotel. I must humor these gentlemen."

I hesitated, thinking I could help him somehow. "Do you need a lawyer? I could call Anna in Moscow and–"

"No. Go to hotel. I will join you for lunch."

I was skeptical, but could only watch as the two men in suits escorted him to the room.

When I got back to the hotel, I was tempted to call Anna,

but I thought of what Max told me. If he needs a lawyer, he probably knows plenty. I decided to wait for an hour or so to see if he returned for lunch as he said he would.

He showed up a few minutes before noon.

"What happened?" I said. "What did they want?"

Max shrugged. "Putin's boys. They want to know what I am doing in Baku. On holiday, I tell them."

"They must know you're interested in the oil fields."

"Of course. They know. I know. But we play this little game. There is nothing they can do. The Azerbaijanis don't like Putin. They think he want to grab oil fields and control economy."

"Control the economy? Could he do that?"

"Sure. He could do anything. But my friends here won't let him. Politically, he can't afford to invade Azerbaijan. So they sell–lease, actually–fields to me, to you, to English. Anybody but him."

I considered this. Anna's warning rang in my head like a bell buoy in a dense fog. "What do we do now?"

"We go to bank."

"Bank?"

"To arrange financing. Appointment at 1400–that's two pm American time."

I began to fidget a bit. We were having a drink on the balcony looking out over the Caspian. I could see the oil derricks just a few miles offshore. "I'm not so sure I'm your man, Max."

"Not my man? Of course you are. I will make you rich."

"Yes...well, I appreciate that, but–I need to think about it."

"Think?"

"Yes. Go home and think. Consult my attorney. The U.S. has very complicated tax laws, you know. Charlotte says–"

"Charlotte?"

"My attorney in Jacksonville. She's an expert on tax law."

Max took a sip of his drink. "Another woman. They run your life."

"Well, some of them are very smart. I have no choice but to depend on them. How long will it take to get loan approval?"

"Three, maybe four weeks."

I thought this over. "Okay. I'll go to the bank with you this afternoon. But then I'm flying back to Florida. That'll give me time to consult with my attorney while the bank here is vetting me. Okay?"

Max grumbled but finally agreed.

CHAPTER 11

Max and I flew back to Moscow the next day and as soon as we arrived at the dacha, I telephoned Anna. There was no answer, so I left a message.

No sooner had we settled in our chairs for dinner than Irina, looking sullen, turned to Max and said something in an accusatory tone. Max looked surprised and said, "Nyet." He continued eating, but Irina persisted. Finally, Max stood up, threw his napkin down, and left the table. Irina and I resumed eating, but of course the tension was high and I couldn't think of anything to say in Russian but "Nice day" and "Good food."

After dinner I went to Max's office and he told me that Irina claimed to smell the scent of another woman on his clothes. He dismissed her accusations as typical of a jealous wife.

"She fire maid while I am gone because she is too pretty." He laughed. "Now we have only fat, old servants."

The next morning I was somewhat relieved to escape the Malenkovsky household as Pyotr took me to the airport.

It was a long flight back to Jacksonville, with changes at Dublin and New York. I was tired and sleepy when I got home, but I called Anna again. This time she answered and apologized for not being available.

I had an engagement in St. Petersburg," she said. The only

number I had for her was her landline in Moscow.

"I will be performing at the Novaya Theatre Thursday through Sunday," she said. "I could fly to Ponte–how do you say it?"

"We pronounce it, 'Ponta Veedra.' But you have to fly into Jacksonville International–which isn't really International. Anyway, you'll have a direct flight from New York."

"I will call you on my cell phone when I arrive. But I'm not sure if it works so well in America."

"If it doesn't, borrow one. Everyone in America has one."

I slept about ten hours and the next morning went to the office.

Elena greeted me with a warm hug. Then she pulled away and looked at me. "What happened to your eye?"

"What's wrong with my eye?"

"It's bloodshot. And you have a bruise on your temple."

My hand went involuntarily to my temple. It was still swollen. "A little accident–I had almost forgotten."

"Sit down, Jake," she said, "and tell me what happened."

We sat down and I told her about the mugging.

"Russia sounds like a dangerous place."

"It happened in Baku. In Azerbaijan."

"Same difference. Are you going back?"

"I don't know. What do you think?"

"I think we ought to be happy with the money we've already made off of Mr. Malenkovsky. Let's not get too greedy."

I smiled. "I seem to recall you complaining about my meager salary at the college."

She frowned. "Well, it *was* meager. Pitiful, even. But the real estate market here is booming. We're both doing well. We should stick to what we know."

This seemed like sound advice. But I knew Elena. "What about that oceanfront house between the two clubs that you always wanted to buy? The one with six bedrooms for not only you, but for the boys now that they're married and their wives are pumping out babies like sausages?"

"That's not a very flattering way to refer to the children of your former stepchildren. Yes, it would be nice. Maybe I could even swing it with a strong year. But Russian oil fields? It sounds a little crazy."

I sighed. "It does, doesn't it?"

"And maybe you ought to sell your shares in that St. Petersburg deal. How much are they worth?"

"I'm not sure. It will depend on the rental income."

"It could be zero. Forget it, Jake. I think Mr. Malenkovsky has taken you for a ride. By the way, I've got an open house I want you to sit on Sunday. Are you available?"

"Jawohl, mein Kapitän!"

"Stop it. It's from two to five. In Old Ponte Vedra. Two point two million. You can read one of your books while you're there."

I did, in fact, read a book at the open house. Or rather, I finished one I had been reading before I left for Russia. It was Nabokov's *Lolita*. In English, of course. Now, I can understand a full-grown man being attracted to a teenager—obviously—since many teenage girls are indistinguishable from full-grown women. But twelve? I mean, no tits, only the first sproutings of pubic hair, button noses—where's the turn-on? I think Nabokov must have been a case of 'arrested development,' as Freud put it. After all, there should be some limit to a man's prurient interests.

But speaking of prurient interests, I nearly got a speeding ticket racing to the airport Monday morning to pick up Anna. I couldn't forget that night in Moscow when her gown kept spilling open and revealing her breasts, then falling to the floor to reveal the most perfectly proportioned female body I'd ever seen. I mean, even her nipples were perfectly round and sharply delineated, like rose petals. Her skin, too, was unblemished, not a mole or a freckle in sight. And the curvature of her hips—well, I could go on and on. Suffice it to say, I was almost at a feverish pitch when I got to the gate.

It doesn't really get cold in North Florida even during the winter months. A light jacket is usually sufficient this time of year. But Anna was dressed more as she would for a Russian winter. She was wearing a cashmere sweater and a short fox fur with matching cap. She looked like a movie star and everyone in the terminal seemed to think so, too. As we were walking towards the baggage claim, some kid, apparently confused about movie chronology, said, "I saw you in *Dr. Zhivago*–I thought you were terrific!" I didn't have the heart to tell him that *Dr. Zhivago* was made in 1965, and Anna wasn't even born then. Nevertheless, she took it as a compliment.

And she looked good in the passenger seat of the car. It reminded me of the days when Elena and I would drive around Ponte Vedra in the Jag on a Sunday afternoon with the top down, her blond hair blowing in the breeze and turning heads everywhere we went.

I wanted to avoid even a hint of impropriety so I booked her into the Inn rather than having her stay at my place. She seemed a bit disappointed at first, but then when the bellhop showed us the room, with a terrific view of the ocean, she was delighted.

"I've never really seen the ocean before," she said. "Not up close like this. I can walk on the beach!"

"We both can," I said.

She smiled and took off her jacket, then her cap. Her hair spilled out over her shoulders and the V-neck sweater she was wearing emphasized the cleavage of her breasts.

"Aren't you hot?" I said.

"Yes," she said, and put her arms around me. "Very hot."

This kind of talk got me excited and I graciously assisted her in taking off her sweater, then her wool skirt.

"We'll have to go shopping tomorrow," I said, "and get you some more Florida-like clothes. Maybe a bikini."

She laughed. "I'm not sure I would feel comfortable in a bikini. People might stare."

"People stare at you anyway. On stage, for instance."

"That's different. I'm fully clothed then."

She says this while she's standing in front of me wearing only panties and a bra. "Would you like to take a shower?"

She put her arms around me again and smiled. "If you promise to scrub my back."

"I promise."

This was one of my promises more easily kept. We lingered in the shower for a while and then moved to the bed. The sliding glass doors were open and we could hear the pounding of the surf on the beach.

I didn't want to get up and dress, but we had a reservation in the club restaurant. Anna got a little annoyed with me as I tried to unbutton her dress after she had buttoned it, slapping my hand away. Finally, I resigned myself to celibacy, at least for the next few hours.

At the restaurant we ordered our meals and I excused myself to go to the men's room. This was an unremarkable event, of course, until I ran into Bob Walker, a fellow Realtor who worked for another company but who I occasionally play golf with.

"Good to see you and Elena are back together again," he said.

I started to correct him, but decided it might be better to humor him. "She's looking good, isn't she?"

"Better than ever. I don't know how she stays so young."

I returned to the table and looked at Anna. She did indeed look like a younger Elena. I wondered if I had some genetic tendency to gravitate towards blondes. My mother was a blonde–maybe that was it. She died when I was very young and I still carry that image of her in my mind–she was thirty-four at the time.

"Why are you staring, Jacob?"

"You remind me of someone."

"Oh? Who?"

"My mother."

She looked at me with a dour expression, then broke into a broad smile. "Was she very pretty?"

"Yes. She was."

"Then I am flattered. Oh–our meals have arrived."

We ate in silence. I regretted having mentioned that she resembled my mother. At least I didn't also mention that she resembled Elena, who resembled Jessica, my former student. I was confused. Was I chasing some chimera, some image stuck in my pre-adolescent brain?

I was beginning to wonder if Anna herself was an illusion.

CHAPTER 12

fter dinner, Anna said she was suffering from jet lag and needed to sleep. So I went back to my place and watched a movie–Buñel's *Discreet Charm of the Bourgeoisie*–and fell asleep as the diners marched down a country road to some unknown destination. This was the third time I've seen this movie and I still don't know why these people are all dressed up and walking to nowhere.

The next morning I got a call from Charlotte–the only brunette in my life.

"Anna is here? Where is she staying?"

"At the club. She was pretty whacked out from the long flight."

"Tell her to call me."

I hung up and called Anna.

"How do you feel this morning?" I said.

"Rested. Why don't you come to the club and we can 'hang out,' as you Americans say, by the pool? I bought a cute little bikini at the club shop this morning."

This got my attention. "Um, great idea. But Charlotte wants you to call her."

"Charlotte? What for?"

"She wants to see you. I thought you were great friends."

"Well...we *are* friends, but I only know her from the few weeks when she was in Moscow."

"Well, she considers *you* a good friend. I'll give you her number and you can call her."

"My cell phone has to go through Moscow. Why don't you call her for me?"

I called Charlotte back and told her about the cell phone problem and she said to tell Anna she wanted to have lunch with her. Could I drop her off at her office?

I felt like the second man on a relay team. I called Anna again and told her about Charlotte's invitation. She seemed reluctant.

"Will you be with us?"

"I'm afraid not–I've got a listing appointment. But I'll drop you off. You and Charlotte have some catching up to do."

"Yes–of course."

I drove Anna into Jacksonville and dropped her off at the front door of Charlotte's office building. It was one of those new high-rises, lots of tinted glass, with a great view of the St. Johns River at the top where Charlotte's office was.

I drove back to Ponte Vedra and just made my listing appointment. This was for one of those houses in a new subdivision a mile or two from the beach. A cookie-cutter. When I told the seller he couldn't get more than 300K for it, he was insulted. I told him to call me when he came to his senses. He practically threw me out of the house.

When I got back to my place, I got a call from Charlotte.

"What happened to her?"

"What happened to who?"

"To Anna. She never showed."

"She didn't? I dropped her off at a quarter till. I'll call her."

I reached Anna at the club. "What happened to you?"

"I'm so sorry, Jacob. I suddenly felt very ill on the elevator. Perhaps it was something I ate last night. Or the jet lag. You must apologize to Charlotte for me."

"How did you get back to the club?"

"A taxi. It's a long ride. And he doesn't take rubles. I had to go to the bank."

I laughed. "The guy had probably never seen a ruble in his life. I should have taken you to the bank myself."

"I feel like an idiot."

"Don't–it's your first time here."

"Well, I was in New York–the taxi driver there *did* take rubles."

"In New York they'll take anything. I'll call Charlotte and smooth things over."

"You're very sweet. I miss you."

"I miss you, too."

Of course it'd been only a couple of hours since I saw her, but in fact I did miss her. In the meantime, I called Charlotte and explained the situation. She suggested that we all have dinner together when Anna felt better.

I got another call. This time it was Max.

"Where are you?" I said.

"Beach. Arrive this morning."

"Well...we'll have to get together sometime."

"How about now?"

"Now?"

"Da. I show you my new robot."

"You bought a robot? What does it do–serve martinis?"

"No. It cleans pool. Miguel serve drinks. Come now."

"Okay."

I drove over to the beach house and once again the Lamborghini was parked in the drive. There was an Hispanic guy waxing it. I parked right next to it hoping that the guy would transfer all that elbow grease to the Jag.

At the door, another Hispanic, a maid, opened it and in broken English directed me to the pool. Max was lying half-prone in a chaise longue wearing his favorite Hawaiian shirt, sucking through a straw inserted into a reamed-out pineapple. He didn't get up, but pulled his shades down a little and peered at me over the top.

"This is the life, no?"

"You've adapted quickly to the Florida lifestyle," I said.

He laughed. "I always adapt. Sit. Miguel will bring you drink."

We watched the robot motor around the pool while waiting for my drink. Just as this was becoming a bit tedious, Miguel appeared with another pineapple.

"What's in it?" I said.

"Rum, vodka, pineapple juice. What else, Miguel?"

"Tequila," Miguel said.

"Ah'" Max said. "The secret ingredient. Muchas gracias, Miguel."

"You are welcome, Señor Malenkovsky."

I watched as Miguel walked back to the house. He was wearing a white waiter's jacket over bermuda shorts and sandals. "Where did you get all these Mexicans?"

"Salvadorans. Miguel and Maria are husband and wife. Ricardo, their son, is polishing the car. They were living like cockroaches in a motel for cockroaches. I rescue them."

"How did you do that?"

"Friends. Take off stupid tie. I have news."

I took off my tie. "Okay. What's up?"

Max explained that the bank and the Ministry of the Interior had approved the loan. All we needed to do was to fly back for the closing.

"I'll have to discuss it with Elena," I said.

"Do that," Max said. "And tell her that one million dollars will be deposited into an escrow account until deal is done."

"One million dollars? What for?"

"For security. If I default, then she is compensated. And you, too."

I wasn't sure about the propriety of this. "And if you don't default?"

"The money–after one year if all goes well–will be distributed to you both. You will not receive salary as CEO. But you still have 20,000 shares, like in St. Petersburg."

"It sounds complicated."

"No–is simple. You tell her."

I didn't finish my pineapple concoction, but put it down and excused myself. When I got out to the driveway, Ricardo was buffing the Jag. It looked like new. I tipped him with a $20 bill and headed for the office.

I explained the deal to Elena and how Max had sweetened the pot.

"One million dollars?" she said. "Into an escrow account?"

"I recommended he set it up with a local attorney. Free of any bureaucratic complications in Azerbaijan."

She stared at me over her desk. "I'll call Richard Haas–he's an expert on foreign transactions." She punched in a few numbers on her cell phone and waited a few seconds for Haas to come on the line. She explained the deal to him. And waited. And waited. Finally, she said, "Okay. Call me back." And hung up.

"Well?" I said.

"He said if Max isn't on the Specially Designated Nationals List, we're good to go."

"What's the Specially Designated Nationals List?"

"An Executive Order signed by Bush back in 2001. After the twin towers attack. It bars any business transactions with suspected terrorists or their sponsors."

"Oh."

We waited for about fifteen minutes while I went to get a

cup of coffee for both of us. When I handed her her cup, she took a sip and looked at me slyly.

"Who's the pretty blonde?"

"What pretty blonde?"

"The one you had dinner with at the club last night. I have my spies, you know."

"Yes, I know. She's, uh, a friend of Charlotte's. From Russia."

"From Russia? And she thought she'd just come all the way to America and pay you a visit?"

"Well, she really came to see Charlotte. They were at a legal conference together a few years ago. But now all she does is sing."

"Sing? What does she sing?"

"Opera."

Elena stared at me as if I had been smoking dope. Then her phone rang.

"The IRS? Okay, Richard. Thanks."

She hung up and turned to me. "Richard says he's not on the list. But we'll have to declare any foreign income. Is he paying you a salary?"

"Not on this one."

She folded her arms across her chest and leaned back in her swivel chair. "I guess it's okay then. Will you have to go back to Azer...Azer..."

"Azerbaijan? I think so. Not sure. Maybe I could sign here and fax the documents to Baku."

"And your Russian girlfriend—what's her name?"

"Anna. But she's not my girlfriend. She's Charlotte's friend."

"Right. Is she going with you?"

"Where?"

"Stop playing games with me Jake. To Azer-whatsit. Bakus."

"Azerbaijan. What do you care?"

"You're my ex. In spite of our past differences, I care about you, Jake. I don't want you to get hurt anymore than you already have been. How's the eye?"

"The swelling's gone down."

"Good. Tell Mr. Malenkovsky I'm on board."

"Will do, Skipper."

I drove back to my condo to change for dinner. When I got there I called Max and told him the good news.

"Horoshow!" Max said. "We leave for Baku tomorrow."

"Tomorrow? Can't we sign the papers and fax them to Baku?"

"Bank want to see you in person. Is required."

I sighed. Anna had just gotten here. I was looking forward to long walks on the beach, a day trip to St. Augustine, a relaxing soak in the tub…"I have a house guest. I can't leave right away."

"House guest? What house guest?"

"Well, not exactly a house guest–she's staying at the Inn. Anna."

"Anna Pavlovna? Why is she–" he cut himself off. Silence. Then, "She is spy. Spy for Putin."

I laughed at this notion. "A spy? She's an opera singer, not a spy. Besides, she hates Putin. He put her in the Lubyanka along with you, remember?"

"Maybe he make deal with her. Pay her big money."

"Don't be silly, Max. She's here to see me. We're in love. I think we're going to get married."

"Married?" A longer silence.

"Not right away," I added hastily. "But eventually. Maybe. Down the road."

"Then she is staying in America?"

"I hope so. For a while, anyway."

"Okay, but we leave tomorrow. Be back in two days."

"Um...okay."

I called Anna and suggested that we have dinner again at the club.

No sooner had I stepped out of the shower than Charlotte called.

"How is she?"

"Anna? She's...she's much better. Just a little upset stomach. Why don't you join us for dinner? At the club."

"I'd be delighted."

While I was getting dressed, I decided that it was time to lay my cards out on the table. That is, tell Charlotte the truth. Anna and I were in love. No more deception, no beating around the bush. It would be painful, but it had to be done.

When I arrived at the dining room, I spotted Charlotte sitting at a table by the window. She waved and the maître d' led the way.

She got up to greet me and gave me a hug. The usual chicken peck on the lips. We sat down.

"Where's Anna?" I said.

"I don't know. I'm a little early, I guess."

I looked at my watch. "Seven on the dot. You're always punctual. Anna's probably still out by the pool." This conjured up an image in my mind of Anna in her new bikini.

"Oh—" Charlotte said, looking over my shoulder. Is that her? She's lost weight."

I turned around. "That's her." I stood up as the maître d' brought her to the table.

The two women stared at each other for a moment.

"How do you do?" Anna said, rather stiffly.

"Anna?" Charlotte said. "It's me—Charlotte. Has it been so long?"

Anna seemed stymied for a moment, then broke out into that warm smile of hers. "Charlotte!" She threw her arms around her. "You've changed your hair."

"No," Charlotte said, disengaging herself. "Well, I guess it's a bit shorter than when I was in Moscow. You look wonderful! And so fit!"

"Well..." Anna took her seat. "I do a lot of swimming these days. Tell me, Charlotte—how is your law practice?"

There's nothing Charlotte would rather talk about than the law. She sat down and launched into the arcane intricacies of a corporate lawsuit she was embroiled in at the moment. Anna and I remained respectfully silent while this was going on until Charlotte paused for a moment to take a breath, then Anna excused herself to go to the powder room.

"I'm afraid I'm boring you two," Charlotte said. "I'm just so wrapped up in this case, I can't think of anything else."

I tried to humor her. "Not at all—it's fascinating. But, you know, Anna isn't practicing law anymore. She's devoted her time lately to her singing career."

"She *does* have a beautiful voice. I never saw her on stage, but she sang for us at dinner one night. It was sublime!"

I told her about Anna's performance at the Bolshoi while I was in Moscow and how she was mobbed by fans and well-wishers. I thought that maybe now was the time to tell her that Anna and I were in love. But I got cold feet.

Anna returned from the powder room looking more radiant than ever.

"Excuse me," she said. "I am still a little unsettled in the stomach."

"Of course," Charlotte said. "It usually takes me two days to get over jet lag. But Jake tells me that you're a big hit now in Moscow. Remember our last night there—the dinner party at the hotel?"

"At the hotel?"

"Yes. At the Metropol, I think it was."

"Oh, yes. The Metropol."

"And you sang happy birthday to one of our group."

"Yes, it was his birthday–now I remember."

Charlotte looked puzzled. "No–it was a 'she', not a 'he.' Carla what's-her-name–the assistant district attorney from New York, remember? The three of us escaped from the group earlier that day and went shopping. You bought her a fur cap for her birthday."

"Oh, yes–Carla. It's been what–three years? I hope she is well."

The rest of the dinner went well as the conversation veered away from their time in Moscow towards Anna's impressions of America, especially Florida. I promised to take Anna to Disney World, though I preferred an excursion to the 'real' Florida like, say, Marjorie Kinnan Rawlings' home in Cross Creek. This idea was met with blank stares by both women.

By the end of the meal, I felt it was time to 'screw my courage to the sticking place,' as Lady MacBeth put it, and tell Charlotte the truth.

"Charlotte," I said uneasily, "Anna and I have something to tell you."

Charlotte looked at Anna for a moment, then back at me. "Yes?"

"Anna and I are in love."

Charlotte's expression did not change. It must have been due to years of awaiting jury verdicts, never expressing disappointment or elation, no matter the outcome. "I'm not surprised. I think you make a lovely couple."

"Charlotte, I–"

"Don't, Jake." She leaned forward and patted my hand. "We've had a wonderful time together, though I'm afraid I've neglected you because of my work. And Anna, you're such a dear–how can I blame you for falling in love with such a charming man as Jake. It's my own fault."

Anna leaned forward and took Charlotte by the hand. "Not at all, Charlotte. It's just one of those things. How can we control our emotions, our passions?"

Charlotte smiled. "We can't, can we? But we can control our friendships. And I want the three of us to always be friends. Jake?"

Now I threw my hand on the pile. "Always."

Charlotte then tossed down the remainder of her wine–and looked out the window. It was dark now, but the moonlight illuminated the surf as it continued to crash onto the beach. "Well, I think we've said all that can be said. I've got a long drive back to San Marco." She rose from her chair.

Anna and I rose, too.

Charlotte gave Anna a hug. I gave them both hugs, trying to be proportionate in my enthusiasm.

Once she was gone, Anna and I sat back down.

"I think she took it quite well," Anna said.

"Yes, she's very stoic. In complete control of her emotions."

Anna put her hand on mine. We were sitting in the same side of the table. "I think you showed great courage and tact, Jacob. But I must say you surprised me. I did not know you felt so strongly about me."

"You are the most fascinating woman I've ever met, Anna. You broke down all my resistance that first night in Moscow."

She smiled at me. "You're very sweet, Jacob." Then she kissed me, a long, lingering kiss in spite of the fact that the dining room was still full and people were staring at us. The pressure of her breast against my ribs began to raise my body temperature–among other things.

"I can't wait to see you in your new bikini," I said.

She laughed. "You can see it tomorrow. We'll have a long walk on the beach."

"Tomorrow? I'm afraid I won't be here tomorrow."

"No? Where are you going?"

"To Baku. Max is here–he wants me to go with him to sign a deal."

"What deal? The oil fields?"

"Yep. It's going to be very lucrative. And I don't really have to do anything. I–"

"Oh, Jacob. I've warned you about Mr. Malenkovsky!"

"Don't worry–Elena's had him checked out. It's okay."

Anna grew very quiet. She gazed out the window into the darkness. Clouds had obscured the moon.

Then she turned to me. "May I come?"

"To Baku? Sure, why not? I'll call Max and–"

"No–don't call him. It'll be a surprise. What time do we leave?"

This was okay with me. Granted, Max thought Anna was some kind of spy, but he was a bit paranoid. I thought of the fact that he had no carpets in his dacha so no one could sneak up on him. Besides, Anna detested Putin as much as he did.

I escorted her back to her room where she brought out her newly purchased bikini. It was pink, one might say shocking pink. The bottom was more like a G-string than a bathing suit, with the sides cut to her hips. The top was two triangular patches attached to each other by spaghetti strings. She walked around in this, first turning one way, then the other, like a fashion model.

"What do you think?" she said.

I was sitting down in a chair trying to conceal my erection. "I think it will attract a lot of attention on the beach."

She came over and sat in my lap. "We'll go someplace remote. Then we both can dispense with bathing suits."

She gave me a kiss.

"Why not tonight?" I said. "There's no one out on the

beach."

She grinned. "All right."

CHAPTER 13

Anna and I fell asleep in her room after our romp in the ocean. But we woke up early and had time for a little more love-making before getting dressed and stopping by my place to pick up a few things.

The St. Augustine airport is a small regional one, but can accommodate large jets. Max's wasn't that large–a Gulfstream something or other–but it was impressive. There was a sitting area, a galley, and cushy seats that folded flat.

Max met us at the steps wearing his Hawaiian shirt, sunglasses, and holding a mixed drink with a little umbrella sticking out of it.

"Doo-bray-oo-tra!" he said. "Good morning. We hop off in ten minutes. Miss McCrory?"

"No, Max," I said. Anna was wearing sunglasses, too. "This is Anna Pavlovna. Remember?"

Max's cheery countenance evaporated. "Miss Pavlovna? You are seeing Jake off?"

"She's coming along," I said. "You don't mind do you?"

Max apparently did mind. He said something to Anna in Russian and she responded in Russian. I couldn't pick up enough of it to get the whole gist of the conversation, but Max said something like, "I don't understand," and Anna said something about wanting to be with me. Then they both said something about the Lubyanka and laughed. Anna followed this up with a disparaging remark about Putin. Then they switched to English.

"We make a party all the way to Baku," Max said. He laughed and motioned us to come aboard. The door was closed, the engines started up, and one of the pilots, doubling as a waiter, handed us a couple of drinks with umbrellas sticking out of them, just like Max's. As we waited on the tarmac to be cleared for takeoff, Max and Anna reverted to Russian and seemed to get along famously.

We were off to Baku.

This time we stopped to refuel in Rome and finally landed in Baku about six a.m. the next morning. As before, an army officer drove us to our hotel and we checked into two rooms, Anna's with a connecting door to our suite. We were able to sleep on the plane so none of us were particularly tired. Max made a phone call and said that the closing would take place at four o'clock that afternoon.

"We take another look at fields," he said. "We not see all of them due to Turkmen boat last time."

So we headed to the yacht basin and set sail for the oil fields.

Along the way, Max pulled out the map and began to trace his finger along the dotted lines that depicted each of the fields, which were marked with a combination of numbers and letters.

"This," he said, "4ADZ9. The largest." He looked out over the bow. "Another ten kilometers. We anchor there and have lunch."

Once we arrived at this furthest oil field, the captain cut the engines and threw out the anchor. Max laid the map out on the table on the rear deck and pointed out various features of the sea floor.

"Is very deep here," He said. "Nine hundred twenty-five

meters."

"How much is that in feet?" I said.

Max took out a calculator. "Three thousand fifty. Very expensive to drill."

Anna seemed uninterested in all of this. "I think I'll go below and change into my swimsuit. This sun is glorious."

Max and I looked up from the map.

"Good idea," I said.

Our eyes followed her as she went to the cabin and disappeared down a hatchway.

"Is good-looking woman," Max said.

"Yes," I said. "And wait till you see her in that swimsuit."

Max flashed a lascivious grin and folded up the map. "We have naked lunch, no?"

"Well," I said. "No. She's my girl, remember?"

"Da. Your girl. Look, but don't touch, no?"

"Exactly."

He laughed uproariously at this and slapped me on the back.

After a few minutes Anna re-emerged, wearing a terry cloth robe over the bikini and headed for the bow. Max took this opportunity to scurry up to the wheelhouse where he could get a better view. I followed.

We stood next to the captain, who was standing next to the first mate, peering out through the windscreen. Anna removed her robe, laid it down on the deck, applied some sun tan oil to her arms, legs, and shoulders, then laid down on her stomach and untied the bikini strings to her top. By this time, the rest of the crew seemed to have remembered that they had certain duties on the bow. But they kept a respectful distance.

Max and I went back to the rear deck where he showed me how he was systematically assembling the oil fields so that they complemented one another. This way, he said, he not only could avoid encroachment from other drillers, but could maximize the efficiency of his own equipment. I poured over the maps, asking him what the various symbols meant and how much each field was expected to yield.

"And who will be your customers?" I said.

"Russia. Europe. India. Tie into pipeline to Central Asia. We are closer than America or Saudi Arabia."

"What about Iran?"

"Big player, but old technology. Sanctions."

This sounded pretty good from a marketing standpoint. I was feeling better about the deal all the time.

At this point, the steward came over and announced that lunch was ready. Max nodded and I went up to the bow and informed Anna.

She looked up. "Oh–I think I fell asleep." She sat up, exposing her breasts, and quickly tied up her top. I noticed that a couple of deckhands who had been polishing the same hardware for the past hour or so got an eyeful.

She decided to go below and change back into her street clothes. Max and I had a drink while we waited for her.

"What take her so long?" Max said. A repast of barbecued shrimp, scallops and sturgeon awaited us, along with dishes of caviar. The steward poured Champagne into our glasses.

Finally, Anna appeared, her hair pulled back into a bun. "Sorry–I couldn't find an outlet for my hair dryer."

"Near the floor," Max said. "Not so convenient."

"Yes–I found one eventually."

Max laughed. "Designer of boat say connections ugly–should be invisible."

"Artists often sacrifice the practical for the aesthetic," she said.

"Aesthetic?" Max said.

Anna translated this word into Russian.

Max offered a toast to the deal and we proceeded with our luncheon. When we finished, the steward and a couple of deckhands cleared away the table and Max sent word to pull up the anchor. He looked at his watch.

Anna went below again and I went up to the bow to watch the crew take up the anchor chain. We were in deep water and it took a while. This done, the captain started the engines. Or tried to. The starter motors just turned over and over. Nothing happened.

The anchor stowed away, Max went up to the wheelhouse. I was still on the bow when he came down again.

"What's wrong?"

"Don't know. Mate go below to find out." He looked anxiously at his watch again

A breeze came up and the clouds took on a darkened hue.

I could see a land mass in the distance which I think was Kazakhstan. There were numerous oil derricks in between. A few ships–gunboats?–plied the waters like sentinels.

"It's a shame to spoil such a beautiful view with ugly towers." Anna had come back on deck and silently nestled against my shoulder.

"Maybe they could cover them up with canvas," I said. "And paint them with pastel colors."

She laughed. "Perhaps you have missed your calling. Have you ever done any painting?"

"Yes," I said. "When I was in kindergarten–finger painting."

She laughed, then looked over her shoulder towards the wheelhouse. "What's wrong–why aren't we moving?"

"Engines won't start. Max went below to look."

Max reappeared and went up to the wheelhouse, preceded by the first mate. I could see him through the windscreen yelling at the captain and waving his arms. Then he came down again.

"What's the problem?" I said.

"First mate is idiot. I call bank, tell them we may be late, but cell phone not work. I use your phone, okay?"

I handed him my phone and he punched in some numbers. While we were waiting for the connection, I looked up at the clouds. They were growing darker and more ominous.

Max suddenly started cursing in Russian. He handed the phone back to me. "Stupid American phones. Not work here."

"Try mine," Anna said.

Max took the phone, punched in the numbers, but with the same result.

"There's a storm brewing," Anna said. Then she said something to Max in Russian. The idea, I guess, was that the storm may have knocked out a cell tower in Baku. We all looked that way and sure enough, it looked like Baku was blanketed with dark clouds.

While Max fumed, Anna and I excused ourselves to go below. It had started raining. But Max stayed out on deck, apparently oblivious, or unconcerned, that he was getting soaked.

"This is kind of weird," I said when we got to the cabin. "First the engines won't work. Then the cell phones. Could they be connected?"

Anna shrugged. "I'm not an engineer." She smiled. "We may have to stay here the night."

Now I smiled. "That wouldn't be so bad, would it? Only we'll miss the closing."

"Closings can be postponed. What does it matter?"

"It matters to Max. He wants to get this thing done. And I'd like to get back to the States. And I'd like you to come with me."

"We'll see."

About this time there was a knock on the door. It was Max. "Sabotage."

"Sabotage?" I said. "What do you mean?"

"Wires. Coil wires, mate say." He took a hard look at Anna. "They are missing."

"Missing? You mean someone pulled them out deliberately?"

"How else? Wires don't fall off by themselves."

I looked at him looking at Anna. "Come on, Max. You don't think Anna climbed down into that greasy engine compartment and ripped out the wires do you?"

Anna looked sour and sat down on the bunk.

"Besides," I said. "How would she know which ones to pull? She's not an engineer, you know."

Max continued staring at Anna for a few moments. Then he sighed.

"Sorry. Could be anyone. Maybe first mate, maybe unhappy sailor, maybe–"

Just then we heard an engine start up. A throaty roar, followed by a second.

"Excuse me," Max said. He went back up on deck.

We got underway and made a beeline for Baku, but after a mile or two the engines quit again. The first mate went below and after another delay of twenty to thirty minutes, the engines roared to life. This happened twice. Finally, we arrived at the marina and tied up at the dock.

Now the cell phones worked. Max called the bank and they told him the closing had been postponed until Monday. A delay of three more days.

So we returned to the hotel.

Max grumbled all the way while Anna and I held hands and looked out at the rain, which was coming down in sheets. As soon as we arrived under the portico, Max pulled out his phone again and called someone. He remained in the car and waved us on.

Anna and I went up to the suite. "I'm so tired," she said. "Do you mind if I take a nap?"

Of course I didn't mind and she left me alone in the living room, wondering what I was going to do for the next hour or so. The champagne from lunch on the boat had worn off and I didn't feel like drinking for a while. So I went out to the balcony–there was a motorized awning you could lower– and stared out at the rain. Anna puzzled me. Sometimes she seemed so warm and affectionate, and sometimes distant, like a stranger. Her English was so impeccable, communication was not a problem. What was it?

As I sat on one of the chairs, the rain splashing off the railing and not quite reaching me, I got a call on my phone. I was glad to see that it was working.

"Hello?" I said. There was a delay between the time I pressed the 'talk' button and when I heard a voice. "Charlotte?"

"Yes, Jake. I've been trying to get a hold of you for the past twenty-four hours. And so has Elena."

"Elena? What for?"

"Is Anna with you?"

"Anna? No, she's taking a nap. Why?"

"She's a spy, Jake. She works for the FSB."

This felt like another mugging. By this time I had wandered into the living room. "A spy? The FSB? How do you know?"

"She's not Anna Pavlovna. Her name is Ekaterina Drubetskova. She was handpicked by Putin because she's a dead ringer for Anna Pavlovna."

"Ekaterina Dru–how do you know this?"

"I know this because the *real* Anna Pavlovna called me from her apartment in Moscow. Which, incidentally, is not the apartment where you met Miss Drubetskova.”

"Not her apartment? This is crazy, Charlotte. I know it was her apartment. I–I spent some time there. And I saw Anna at the Bolshoi. Singing. Could this 'dead ringer,' as you say, also have a great operatic voice?”

"You saw the real Anna Pavlovna at the Bolshoi. They tapped her phone and rerouted it to Miss Drubetskova's. You never spoke to or met Anna–you only saw her onstage.”

This seemed incredible. And far-fetched even for a conspiracy theory. "Where are you?”

"I'm in Baku.”

"Baku? What in the world are you doing here?”

"Anna asked me to come. And Elena, too.”

"Good God! What for?”

"To save you from going to prison. Or worse. Wait–here's Elena.”

Elena came on the phone. "Jake, you've been duped. Max has made you a pawn in his effort to steal these oil fields.”

"Steal them? Doesn't he have the money?”

"Yes. And he's using some of it to bribe the Azerbaijani authorities. Jake, you've got to get out of that hotel and come to ours. We're at the Marriott.”

"I can't–Max will wonder what happened to me. And Anna–you say her name is Ekaterina?”

"That's it.”

"What am I going to tell her?”

"You'll think of something.”

CHAPTER 14

I felt like a fool. How could I have fallen for such a scheme? Now all of Anna's little excuses and sudden headaches made sense. But how would I extricate myself? Just walk out?

While I was contemplating my next move, Max appeared. He suddenly seemed in good spirits.

"Horoshow!" he said. "Closing is moved up to Saturday. Bank closed but they open for me."

"That's great—what time?" I sat in a chair pretending to take an interest in an English language magazine.

"Three o'clock. Where's Anna Pavlovna?"

"In her bedroom. She was tired."

Max went to the bar. "Sorry I suspect her of spying. She no friend of Putin. Want a drink?"

"No, thanks."

He shrugged his shoulders and poured himself a glass of vodka. This time he tossed a couple of olives in along with a touch of vermouth. I had taught him how to make martinis and he loved them.

"I've been thinking, Max," I said, flipping the pages of the magazine.

Max came over and sat down in a chair opposite mine. "Thinking? About what?"

"About the deal. How are you going to keep Putin out of

this? He's a very powerful man."

"I told you–the Azerbaijanis don't like him. They afraid he take control of economy if he control oil fields. They like me better."

"But couldn't he order the Azerbaijanis to stop the deal?"

"How?" He took a sip–not a gulp–of his martini. I had taught him well. "Putin very bad man–but he like to follow law whenever possible. There is no law say he can interfere in government of Azerbaijan. Not without invasion of troops."

"So why can't he do that?"

"NATO."

"NATO? Azerbaijan is a member of NATO?"

"Not exactly. 'Partner in Peace,' I think they call it. You sure you not want martini? How James Bond say it? 'Shaken, not stirred.'"

"No, thanks. So NATO would come to the defense of Azerbaijan if Russia invaded?"

Max shrugged. "Maybe. Not full member. But Azerbaijan send troops to Kosovo, Iraq, Afghanistan. NATO feel obligated."

I contemplated this. If Putin couldn't stop this closing how could the girls do it?

I rose from my chair. "I think I'll go for a walk."

"Walk? It still raining outside."

"I like to walk in the rain."

He stared at me for a few moments, then took another sip of his martini. "Okay. Go for walk in rain. Come back, take hot shower, then we go to dinner. I know this little Armenian restaurant–"

At this point, 'Anna' appeared at the door to her bedroom. She looked sleepy-eyed and was wearing a terry cloth bathrobe supplied by the hotel.

"How was your nap?" I said.

"Restful. Kak dela, Max?"

"Horoshow. You like a martini?"

"Sure."

Somehow I couldn't just walk out now.

We all sat around and had a drink and I tried to pick up on the conversation between Max and 'Anna.' They seemed to have suddenly become good friends.

Later, we went out to Max's little Armenian restaurant and had a dish called Horovats, which was a kebab made from pork, along with eggplant, green peppers and various spices. Afterwards, as a sort of dessert, we had something called Byoreks, a pastry stuffed with cheese. Of course Max ordered plenty of wine, a pretty good red from the now independent country of Georgia.

All during this meal, Max and 'Anna' continued to converse in Russian. Occasionally, she would translate for me. I just nodded without interest for they seemed mainly to be talking about American movies, which, ironically, I had never seen.

Max, it turned out, was a big James Bond fan, while 'Anna' preferred John Wayne and westerns generally. I liked French comedies and adaptations of British classics. They both looked at me with blank stares when I offered up *Tom Jones* as my favorite film.

That night 'Anna' and I lay in bed with little to say to each other. Neither of us seemed much interested in sex. She teased me a little about my traditional tastes in movies and books (Dostoevsky was a 'religious fanatic,' she said) and turned away and went to sleep. I lay awake wondering if Charlotte had her information right. How did Putin–or the FSB–make the switch? Why didn't I see the 'real' Anna Pavlovna as I was coming and going to the apartment? And that night at the opera–I was mesmerized by her performance and went backstage to see her afterwards. On the other hand, I hadn't actually seen her then. It was too crowded and that guy in the dark suit—an FSB agent?—handed me a note saying she would meet me in the bar. That was it? This, this Ekaterina Drubetskova slipped into the bar and the real Anna simply went home?

I was confused and skeptical. I wondered if I could trust anybody, including Charlotte. I didn't get much sleep that night.

The next morning, I got up early–'Anna' was still sleeping and apparently so was Max—and went out onto the balcony where I sat down and had a cup of coffee. The rain had quit during the night and I watched the sun rise over the Caspian like a great orange ball against a cloudless but hazy blue-green sky. These unusual colors reminded me that I was in a remote and very different part of the world.

I got a call on my cell phone. It was Charlotte.

"Why didn't you come to the Marriott last night?"

"I couldn't get away. We went to dinner and when we got back, it was late."

"Well, things have changed. Anna called the closing agent after I called you and told him that Max had bribed somebody in the Ministry so he could shut the consortium out of the deal."

"What consortium?"

"The British-American—never mind. The point is the agent stone-walled it, saying that Anna must be crazy."

"Maybe she *is* crazy. How does she know all this, anyway?"

"She has friends. Her only option now is to go to a media organisation and tell them about it. In other words, to go public."

"Why doesn't she just call up Putin and tell him? He could put a stop to it with one phone call."

"And then he would get the oil fields. That is, if the Azer-baijanis felt intimidated enough—and he could sweeten the pot."

"Who *does* she want to get it?"

"The consortium."

"Why? Does she work for the consortium?"

"No. She just wants the deal to be aboveboard. Before Putin jailed her, she was a crusader against corruption, remember?"

"I remember. I think. Apparently I don't even know the woman."

"Well, you can meet her today at ten o'clock."

"At ten? Where?"

"Koala Park. Gotta go."

She hung up.

I didn't even know where Koala Park was. I pulled out one of the hotel maps and quickly located it. A short taxi ride. The closing was set for 3 p.m. I wondered what Max was planning to do until then. I was soon to find out.

"Doo-bray-ootra!" He appeared at his bedroom door wearing a silk dressing gown, tying the sash around his waist. He seemed to never have hangovers no matter how much he had had to drink the night before.

"Doo-bray-ootra," I said.

"Your Russian is getting better. What you want for break-fast?"

"Oh—whatever you're having."

He looked towards 'Anna's door. "Where is Sleeping Beau-ty?"

"Sleeping," I said, idiotically.

"Interesting woman. I order blintzes, bacon, coffee. Ok?"

"Fine with me."

I wondered how I was going to make my escape. "What are you planning to do until the closing, Max?"

"Read newspaper. Lunch in hotel restaurant. Bank."

"Bank? But it's not until three o'clock."

"Need to be there early. Wire transfer from Moscow."

"Oh."

"You come with me?"

"Well, uh, I don't think you need me for that. I think I'll explore the city a little. I haven't really seen it in the daytime."

Max laughed. "Safer, no? Not so many robbers."

About that time 'Anna' appeared in her terry cloth robe. After the usual exchange of pleasantries in Russian and English, she said:

"I think I'll go shopping. There's a festival going on."

"Da," Max said. "Cheap. Everything tax free."

"You'll have to tell me how to get there."

"Is everywhere. Look for signs in windows."

Now the escape problem was solved. Max would go to the bank, 'Anna' to the shopping malls, and I to Koala Park.

After breakfast, 'Anna' and I walked out of the hotel lobby together.

"Are you going to the closing?" I said.

"I think not."

"Why not?"

She smiled, rather patronizingly, I thought.

"Because Mr. Malenkovsky may find my presence awkward."

"Awkward? In what way?"

She leaned over and gave me a kiss on the cheek. "I'll see you this afternoon at the hotel. Five-ish."

Then she walked briskly away, presumably to one of the malls.

Rather than take a taxi–these are curious conveyances in Baku, upholstered in handwoven carpets–I decided to walk.

It was only a few blocks to the park. I stopped to look in at a few stores with the signs Max mentioned announcing they were officially endorsed by the festival and promising the redemption of the Value Added Tax. I saw a really nice leather sports jacket for a ridiculously low price and bought it.

About a block from the park I heard loudspeakers and a woman's voice rattling off something in Russian. It sounded like a political rally. As I got closer, I saw a growing mob of people congregating around a platform—a bunch of hastily assembled packing crates, as it turned out—and three women, one of then holding a bullhorn. The one holding the bullhorn looked like 'Anna.' The other two, animated and cautious at the same time, were Elena and Charlotte.

After this Anna finished her spiel, Charlotte took the bullhorn from her:

"Mr. Malenkovsky is a criminal attempting to steal your oilfields," she said. "He has bribed your officials and seeks to control your government."

Then the woman who I assumed to be the real Anna Pavlovna took the bullhorn back and repeated in Russian what Charlotte had just said in English. I also heard her mention the name 'Putin.' Apparently, they were implicating both in this scheme and were appealing to the English-speaking media as well as the Russian in order to maximize news coverage. Most Azerbaijanis spoke Russian, so they understood what was being said.

As this Anna continued evermore excitedly in Russian, the crowd grew and began shouting in support of her.

But before long, a couple of dozen helmeted policemen waded into the crowd swinging batons. Anna Pavlovna kept on shouting in Russian. The cops eventually mounted the platform and snatched the bullhorn away. Then they grabbed all three women and hustled them off to a police van.

This all happened so fast I didn't even have a chance to make my presence known to the girls. And what was I supposed to do–fight off a small army of riot police?

The van rolled off down the street and turned on a siren that sounded like a lovesick moose. The crowd dispersed.

I turned to a guy next to me and asked in stilted Russian: "Ga-da tur-ma?"

"The jail? Near the railway station, on Nizami Street."

"You're an American?"

"Yes. Your Russian is terrible. I work for the American Embassy. You know these women?"

"I do."

"Well, they're in a bit of trouble. Here, take my card. Call me if I can help."

He walked away and I looked at his card:

Jonathan Meyers
Vice-Consul
American Embassy
111 Azadliq Avenue
Baku, Azerbaijan
+994 12 488 33 00

CHAPTER 15

I found the Nizami prison easily enough, but was met with an officious character at the reception desk who spoke neither Russian nor English. After some shouting and arm-waving, I finally decided this was getting me nowhere and produced Mr. Meyers' business card. I guess he thought I was Jonathan Myers, and the card looked very impressive, so he motioned me through a door to his right. The signs were in Azerbaijani.

A second official looked at the card and said to another one standing guard at a heavy steel door, "Amerikanski." This guard opened the door, went inside and after a minute or two, Charlotte and Elena appeared. They looked very relieved to see me, but said nothing. Then the second official indicated that we should have a seat among the chairs facing his desk. He looked at the card, then at me, then picked up the phone and dialed a number. After a short conversation, he looked at the girls and said,

"You are free to go."

"What about Anna Pavlovna?" Charlotte said as she stood.

"Miss Andropova is a Russian national. She must apply to the Russian Embassy."

"But has she been allowed to call them?"

The official shrugged his shoulders. "Go now."

I hustled both of them out of the building before they could be re-arrested. Out on the street, we all hugged one another.

Elena sighed with relief. "I thought we might be in there for the rest of our lives!"

"We've got to help Anna," Charlotte said.

"You could call the Russian Embassy for her," I said.

"How? I don't speak Russian."

"Somebody there will speak English."

We took a cab to their hotel where we turned on the TV while Charlotte phoned the Russian Embassy. There was already a video of the fracas at Koala Park on the screen and a commentator mentioned "Maximilianovich Malenkovsky" several times. I picked up enough of it to gather that Max had also been arrested.

Elena and I sat down on the sofa.

"Where's your Russian girlfriend?" she said.

"Out shopping."

"Have you told her you're on to her?"

"Not yet."

"Poor Jake."

By this time, Charlotte had gotten hold of someone at the Russian Embassy who could speak English.

"Can't you do anything for her? She's a Russian citizen and under your constitution she has the right of free speech." Charlotte nodded as she listened to the official. Then she hung up.

"He says that she will have to appear before the Prosecutor General and pay a fine for demonstrating without a permit."

"A fine? Then we'll pay it for her."

"Of course," Charlotte said. "But we'll have to find out where the Prosecutor General's office is."

"Call Mr. Myers. He'll know where to go and who to talk to."

"Good idea."

I looked at my watch. "I'd better get back to my hotel."

Elena gave me a sly look. "To meet your paramour?"

I rose from the sofa. "She's not my paramour anymore. A spy! I can't believe it."

"You're so gullible, Jake," Elena said. "Especially when a pretty woman bats her eyelashes at you."

"Just like you did in geography class."

"In geography class?" Charlotte said. "You've known each other that long?"

"Seems longer," Elena said. "We lost touch after high school. Jake returned after teaching in Pongo Pongo for a few years and seduced me with his boyish charm."

"Actually, it was Pago Pago. Samoa."

"Whatever."

Charlotte smiled. "The native women must have found him irresistible."

"And vice-versa," Elena said. "He particularly liked the fact that they walked around topless."

"Okay, okay," I said. "You two can dissect my character and laugh all you want while I go back to the hotel."

Elena stood and gave me a kiss on the cheek. "Don't be so sensitive, Jake. We're just teasing you. And we want to protect you."

"Well, you've done that, I guess. Now I'm sadder but wiser."

"Poor Jake."

"Charlotte—keep me posted as to the fate of the real Anna Pavlovna. I'd like to meet her before we leave."

"Be careful, Jake," Elena said. "Remember, she's a professional."

"Miss Drubetskova? I just hope she doesn't carry a stiletto in her purse."

I walked back to my hotel, trying to think along the way what I was going to say to Anna—or rather Ekaterina. 'Ekaterina.' An awkward name. Hardly falls trippingly off the tongue.

She was in her room when I arrived at the suite, modeling a dress she had bought in front of a mirror.

"What do you think?"

"It looks lovely."

"Indian silk. Only fifty manats before the tax rebate. Incredible!"

As I sat on the edge of the bed, she extracted some other items from the shopping bags. A couple of sweaters, some panty hose, a negligée. She modeled the negligée for me, pressing it over her dress, tucking it tightly beneath her breasts.

"And this?"

"Very sexy."

She pouted for a moment and then came over and kissed me. "Jake–you seem so sad."

"Don't you want to know about the closing?"

"Oh, yes. How did it go?"

"Canceled. Max has been arrested."

She clicked her tongue against her palate. "Poor Max. Of course I warned you–he has a history of shady dealings."

"You did warn me, didn't you? But there's something you didn't warn me about."

"What's that?"

"You."

She looked at me with a tilt of her head that suggested no further discussion was necessary. "I'll have to find room for all of these new clothes. I don't expect that you'll want to help."

"No, Ekaterina. I don't."

She pretended not to hear the name, and started pulling clothes out of a drawer.

"Ekaterina Drubetskova–isn't that your real name?"

"It will do as well as any other."

"How many aliases do you have?"

She ignored this.

"Aren't I entitled to some explanation?" I said.

She had her back to me, then turned around. "I suppose so. You're a sweet man and I don't want to hurt you, but all you need to know is what I've already told you–Mr. Malenkovsky is a bad man."

"And Mr. Putin isn't?"

"I know no more about Mr. Putin than what I read in the papers. Like you."

"Do you work for the FSB?"

"I have a job. At the Ministry of Culture."

It was clear that she wasn't going to reveal anything more.

"So it's over," I said.

"Our relationship? I'm afraid so. You'll go back to America and I'll go back to my job in Moscow."

I really couldn't restrain myself any longer. I got up and grabbed her by the shoulders. "Don't you have any feelings for me at all? Anna–or Ekaterina–"

"You can call me Katya–if you release your hands from my shoulders."

I released her. "Katya–can you be so cold-hearted? I fell in love with you–all of you–even the lies you made up. I could forgive you even for that if–"

"Yes?"

"If I could believe you had some genuine affection for me. All those nights in bed–"

"That was the easiest part. The hard part was listening to your drivel about Dostoevsky and Shakespeare and Sigmund Freud. Freud! A degenerate Jew. You Americans will believe anything!"

Now it was my turn to smile. "The decadent West, eh? I forgot that you were born in the Soviet era. Old myths die hard, don't they?"

She glared at me for a moment, then went back to her packing. "Excuse me—I have things to do."

I left and went to the balcony and stared out over the Caspian thinking of...nothing, really. That's the way I felt. My life, especially my relationships with women, had amounted to nothing. So much time, energy, hopes and despair—at least despair involved some feelings—came once again to nothing.

When she finished packing she came out into the living room and went to the door. I could hear by her footsteps, even on the soft carpet, exactly where she was though I didn't turn around. She paused at the door, set her bags down, and came to the middle of the room. The sliding glass doors to the balcony were open.

"Jake," she said. "If you are ever in Moscow again—come see me. My name—Ekaterina Drubetskova—is in the book."

I turned around. She was smartly dressed now, in a sort of business suit. But her beauty shined through. Even Elena in her youth was never so beautiful. "Are you sure?"

"Of course I'm sure. I have my career at the Ministry, but I'm still a woman. And Russian men are such pigs."

"And American men?"

"Naïve, but kind. Like you."

I felt like rushing over to her and taking her in my arms, but that was for fairy tales. She had just given me a dose of reality that inoculated me from future dreams. "Goodbye, Katya."

She hesitated a moment, there was a slight quiver of her lips, and she headed for the door. I suppose I should have opened it for her, but I didn't want to get too close to her again. Burned once...

She picked up her bags, and with one last look over her shoulder said, "Goodbye, Jake."

CHAPTER 16

We paid a 'fine' to get the real Anna Pavlovna out of jail and the four of us flew back to Moscow, where we stayed overnight in Anna's apartment. It was the same building, only on the seventh floor, three below the phony 'Anna's on the tenth. The FSB had apparently done their homework, duplicating the real Anna's furnishings, even the photograph of her mother being fêted by Stalin. I also discovered that there were not one, but two elevators in the building. Katya—I suppose I should call her by her real name now—always took the one at the south end of the building, while the real Anna used the one at the north end. This is why we never crossed paths.

The resemblance between the two was remarkable, only a slight difference in their body types. The real Anna was about ten or fifteen pounds heavier, which corresponded to the photo in Charlotte's living room. She also was not exactly blemish-free as Katya was. This Anna had a dark mole on her neck, just below her left ear. And unlike Katya, her front teeth were closely spaced—no gap. Nevertheless, she was a charming woman and after I got over the sense of déja vu, I was able to relax a little. Still, I had the feeling that I could reach out and touch her and somehow she would respond the way Katya did during our first encounter.

There were two bedrooms, so that Anna Pavlovna slept in

hers and Charlotte and Elena slept in the other while I was assigned to the sofa. After unpacking the necessities, we all sat down in the living room and had a glass of champagne.

"I cannot thank you enough for coming to my rescue, Jacob," Anna said. "That jail in Baku was filthy and damp. The Lubyanka was a luxury hotel by comparison."

"It was actually Elena and Charlotte who rescued you, Anna. And I might have ended up in jail, too, if it hadn't been for them."

"Poor Mr. Malenkovsky," Anna said. "I'm afraid he's going back to the Lubyanka."

"What will they do to him?" Elena said.

"I suppose there will be a trial of sorts, so that Mr. Putin can claim that he's cleaning up the corruption in Russia. But no one will believe that and Mr. Malenkovsky will no doubt spend the next few years in prison. They may even transfer him to one in Siberia to make it more difficult for his friends to procure his release."

This talk of prison cast a pall over the conversation for a few seconds, but it was Charlotte who broke through it. "When can we hear you sing, Anna?"

Anna brightened. "I'm scheduled to sing at the Bolshoi Friday night. I should be honored if you can attend."

"Of course we can attend," Charlotte said. "It's only another day or two. That's if you can put up with us for that long."

"I owe you all an immense amount of gratitude," Anna said. "We're a bit cramped here, but I think it may be more comfortable than many of the hotels in Moscow. And of course the price is right!"

We all laughed at this and I offered to take everyone out to dinner.

"How about the Pushkin?" I said.

"Very expensive," Anna said.

"I'm an oil man, remember?"

Elena rolled her eyes at this comment, but the others laughed and we finished our champagne before heading out for the Pushkin. There was no smashing of glasses against the fireplace this time, however.

The next day Elena and Charlotte and I went shopping, and after tagging along through the GUM department store and a few boutiques in the Arbat, I excused myself and went first to the Tolstoy Museum, then to the Pushkin where I met up with the girls again.

When Friday night arrived we settled into our seats at the Bolshoi as the orchestra played the overture to *Boris Godunov*. This is a rather dark, even morose opera by Mussorgsky in which Boris, the Czar, convinces himself that Gregory, a pretender to the throne, has risen from the dead and now seeks to depose him. It seemed to have some likeness to *Hamlet*.

Anna Pavlovna didn't appear until the third scene. She played the Czar's daughter, Xenia. It was a small role, but she sang with the angelic voice I remembered from her role as Tatiania in *Eugene Onegin*. It was somehow ethereal and sexy at the same time. Though I knew this was Anna and not Katya Drubetskova, I couldn't help but see the two melded into one woman.

"Jake," Charlotte whispered in my ear, "you're trembling." She was sitting to my left with Elena to her left and with her hand on mine.

"It's just a draft."

"There's no draft in here. Are you all right?"

"I'm fine."

"You're crying."

I wiped the incriminating tear away. "Anna's voice—it reminds me of my mother." This was a lie—my mother never sang to me or anyone else as far as I know.

Charlotte patted my hand. "You're a sensitive soul, Jake. Men should cry more often."

I didn't have an answer for this, and decided that it was best not to disillusion Charlotte, who seemed to buy into the idea that I was pining away for my deceased mother. I didn't have the heart to tell her that I was pining away for Katya.

CHAPTER 17

Charlotte, Elena and I flew back to Florida on the same flight. The two of them seemed to get along famously, occasionally glancing at me and sharing some joke at my expense. I happened to be sitting across the aisle from them, and with the whine of the jet engines I didn't catch everything that was said. But it was clear that I was the butt of their jokes. Elena would, from time to time, lean across the aisle and pat me on the arm. "Dear Jake," she would say. It was as if I were a child who had fallen off his bicycle and suffered a few cuts and bruises, nothing more.

Back in Ponte Vedra, I found it difficult to settle into my old routine. The real estate business was slowing down and I felt it all to be a bore. I thought about applying for a teaching job–somewhere like Alaska, where they had never heard of my little indiscretion at Ponce De Leon College. But then they were bound to find out unless I omitted that particular job from my resumé.

About a week later, Elena called me into her office.

"I just got a call from Charlotte," she said. "She just got a call from Anna."

"Oh?" I said, hardly paying attention.

"Anna says that Mr. Malenkovsky's real estate deal in St. Petersburg has been declared null and void–therefore, you are no longer CEO of the corporation because there is no corporation."

I restrained myself from yawning. "I'm not surprised. There are no shares, either, then."

"Correct."

"What's happened with the oil fields?"

"Some consortium snapped them up."

"At least Mr. Putin didn't get them."

"Who cares who got them?"

"What about the escrow money?"

"It's been returned to Mr. Malenkovsky. But meanwhile the Russian government claims that it was obtained fraudulently and has frozen his bank account."

"Then Putin wins after all."

"Yes. But that's not all–Mr. Malenkovsky called me."

"Did he? What did he have to say?"

"He wants me to sell his beach house. He needs the money, he says."

"Obviously."

"But Jake–it's a monstrosity. We can't sell it quickly."

"Also obvious."

"You're not helping."

"Sorry. But what can *I* do?"

"You can help me sell it."

"How?"

"I've been thinking. It's actually a very pretty house–it just needs renovating. Will you go down there with me so we can see what needs to be done?"

"Sure. But who's going to pay for the renovations? Not Max."

Elena exhaled slowly, leaned back in her chair, and stared at the ceiling. She seemed to be deep in thought. Suddenly she sat up and leaned forward. "Jake!"

Having almost fallen asleep, I was startled. "What?"

"*We* could buy it!"

"*We*? What are you talking about? I can barely make the mortgage payments on my condo. My car's more than ten years old and–"

"Your trust fund."

"My trust fund? I can't touch that until my father dies. And he looked the picture of health the last time I saw him. New girlfriend. Flying down to the Bahamas with her–"

"It's collateral. With my equity in the business we could swing it."

"And what–take it as joint tenants? No, Elena, it would never work. You downstairs and me upstairs? Or vice-versa? And how would we make the payments?"

"Don't you see? We wouldn't live in it–we'd flip it. Malenkovsky is desperate for cash."

I considered this. "How much would it cost to renovate it?"

"A hundred grand. Tops. We could do the painting and decorating ourselves. Buy it for three mil, flip it for six. A profit of 1.5 mil each."

"Minus expenses."

"Minus expenses."

I sighed. "I don't know, Elena."

"Of course you don't–you're never willing to take risks. Except where women are concerned."

She rose from her desk. "Come on. Let's take a look. If you still have cold feet, I'll find another investor."

We drove down to South Ponte Vedra in my Jag with the top down, just like in the old days, with Elena's blond hair flowing in the breeze. The Jag is somewhat of a tight fit, so we were often touching, Elena occasionally putting her hand on my arm to caution me about someone pulling out of a driveway or a tortoise taking his time to cross the road. There's a tree canopy along this stretch that seems almost like a tunnel–a tunnel of love, I used to say to Elena, only half jokingly. In those days we *were* in love. The proximity of her body, the slight jiggle of her breasts as we hit a bump, her cautionary hand on my arm–all made me think that maybe those days could come back...

I parked the car in the drive and like the gentleman that I am, went around to Elena's side to open the door for her. Only she had already opened it herself. She looked at me for a moment, then shook her head and got out of the car.

"Old school Jake," she said. "It's not necessary, but I appreciate the thought."

We approached the front door as Elena fished in her purse for the key. She had retained one so that she could enter in an emergency while Max was in Russia. But before she could insert the key in the lock, the door opened. Standing there to greet us was Miguel.

"Welcome, Señora McCrory." He nodded to me. "Señor Jake." He opened the door wide and extended his arm towards the living room as if to say the house was ours.

"We didn't know you were still here, Miguel," Elena said. "Mr. Malenkovsky isn't coming back, you know."

Miguel's eyes grew large. "No?"

"Not for a long time, anyway," Elena said. "Have you been paid this month?"

"Si. For three months. But Señor Max–he is in trouble?"

"Quite a bit," Elena said. "But don't worry–you can stay here until the house is sold. And if it takes longer than three months, Mr. Gavronski and I will make sure that you and Maria are paid."

I raised my eyebrows at this, but I could hardly object. Where would they go? I noted that Maria was standing just inside the living room, wiping her hands on her white apron. Cooking smells wafted in from the kitchen–onions and spices

and grilled meat. Miguel seemed to notice that my nose was
in the air, nostrils flared.

"You will stay for lunch?" he said.

"Thank you, Miguel," Elena said, "but we have business
to tend to. If you don't mind, we'll take a look around. Just
enjoy your lunch and don't mind us."

Miguel nodded, Maria looked gravely concerned, and Elena
and I strolled through the living room trying not to blanch at
the atrocious artwork and the garish décor.

After a thorough assessment of each room in the house—
to which Elena frequently applied her measuring tape—we
walked out onto the patio and sat near the pool.

"Well," I said. "What do you think?"

She looked back at the house as if she could see through the
walls. "I think it's doable. Why don't we take a stroll on the
beach? The tide is out."

We walked down to the dunes and used the walk-over to
get to the beach. The air was crisp and cool, with a steady
breeze of about ten to fifteen knots. A couple of wind-surfers
were taking advantage of the conditions, manipulating their
sails and guiding the boards through the breaking waves. We
walked down to the water's edge where Elena slipped off her
shoes and allowed the water to run over her feet. She shook
off some sea foam that had accumulated between her toes.

"It would be so nice to live here," Elena said.

"Well, who doesn't want to live on the ocean?" I said. "But
even if you have the purchase price, the overhead is prohibi-
tive."

"It wouldn't take long to sell it. The typical buyer in this
range doesn't sweat the maintenance."

"I guess not."

We walked along the beach for a few minutes, me thinking of how nice it would be to cozy up in bed with Elena

every night and Elena–I knew her–thinking about how nice it would be to throw parties so she could show the place off along with her designer dresses and the jewelry she had accumulated from her previous husbands. Unfortunately, I had only managed to cough up enough money for some pearl earrings for our engagement–earrings that she still wore.

"I think we should knock down the wall between the kitchen and the dining room," she said, as if having a revelation. "Open it up. It would have a natural flow."

"Good idea," I said.

"And all that felt wall covering–ugh! We could rip that down and paint the walls different pastel colors–cerulean blue for the living room, salmon for the dining room, rose for the master bedroom–"

"Elena–"

"Hmm?"

"Don't you think you're getting ahead of yourself?"

"Ahead? Of course I'm getting ahead of myself. You've got to get ahead of yourself if you're going to envision the future. Don't you ever envision the future, Jake? Or is it just immediate pleasure with you?"

I took this as the insult it was intended to be. "You didn't seem to be adverse to immediate pleasure that first night on our honeymoon in the jacuzzi. In between sips of champagne."

She frowned. "That was your idea. Not mine."

"But you enjoyed it."

"Of course I enjoyed it. But Jake, dear, there's more to life than sex."

"Like what?"

She shrugged her shoulders and walked on. "You're hopeless."

I followed. "Seriously–like what? Sex is at the basis of everything. It brings two people together who otherwise have little in common; it gives both partners comfort and intimacy, which leads to love. And ultimately the propagation of the human race! What could be more important?"

"You've got it backwards. *Love* leads to intimacy, not the other way around. Did your 'intimacy' with that little co-ed at the college lead to love? No. Did your affair with the phony 'Anna' lead to love? Of course not. Those two little sordid incidents—not to mention a half a dozen others that I won't mention—only led to disaster and all for the sake of a few moments of pleasure. You still haven't learned anything, Jake."

"And what have you learned, Elena? That money is the Holy Grail? What has it bought you—or will buy you? More clothes, a new Mercedes, a beach house to impress your friends? How is that a more noble endeavor than sex?"

"The only thing 'noble' about sex is that it produces children, Jake. For all of your philandering, you haven't produced any children. Did you ever see that urologist my father recommended? I think you're sterile."

As I tried to gather my thoughts for a rebuttal, she bent over to pick up a shell in the sand. When she does this, her back and her rear end form a sort of reverse 'S' with her skirt pulled tightly over the buttocks and emphasizing the cleavage, which runs almost all the way to the base of her spine. I was partly angry at what she said about my being sterile and partly aroused by the posture she was in. I felt a sudden impulse to reach under her skirt and yank her panties down and drill her right there on the beach in broad daylight. But the wind surfers were gathering up their sails and approaching us. And Elena had a way of defusing my impulses.

She stood and held up the scallop shell she had just unearthed from the wet sand. "See that, Jake? Look carefully. What do you see?"

I looked. It was a very pretty shell, perfectly symmetrical with grooves fanning out from its base, copper and white on the outside and rosy pink on the inside. "A shell. Very pretty."

"Beautiful, I would say."

"Okay. Beautiful."

"And except for a few shells on the beach like this, beauty costs money." She gestured towards the breaking waves. "To see this every morning when you wake up costs money. Sure, you can see it once in a while when you bring the kids down to a public access and frolic in the surf for a couple of hours. But then you have to go home to your squalid little bungalow and look at the walls with cheap reproductions and dirty fingerprints. Beauty, real beauty, lasts, Jake. Sex doesn't. When the hormones start to go—and they already have, for me at least—then sex is of secondary interest."

I couldn't think of a rebuttal to this right away and we walked on for a while in silence.

After a few minutes, she stopped suddenly and turned to me. "Jake...I'm sorry about what I said about your being sterile. I'm sure it's not true. And I didn't mean to say that our time together wasn't good—it was. Even blissful at times. But..."

"But I spoiled it, didn't I?"

We continued walking. "It was as much my fault as yours. I wasn't always available to you. I mean in the way you wanted me to be."

"No...It *was* my fault. But Elena—sometimes I just can't help myself with women. What can I do about it?"

"Just grow up, Jake. Like I'm having to do." Then she laughed, seemed to rebuke herself, looked at the shell she had found for a moment, and put it in her purse.

CHAPTER 18

Elena spent the next week or so lining up loans and contractors to renovate the beach house. And she was right about the trust fund. My banker wasn't aware that I had one, but when he found out it amounted to seven figures—it surprised me as much as it did him—he granted me a construction loan without Elena having to hock her jewelry. But she dealt with the contractors and initially, at least, I had little to do. So I played golf. Golf is a great escape from the real world. And you meet interesting people sometimes.

The club is actually open to non-members who stay at the Inn. And being very expensive, you get some high-flyers from time to time. A good way to get business without actually having to work for it.

On Saturday I booked a tee time as a single since my usual partner—Bob Walker—had had a heart attack while I was in Russia. He survived it, they put in a couple of stents, and he was recuperating. I visited him in the hospital and you would never know he had had anything more serious than a nosebleed.

Anyway, the club pro put me with a woman who he said was a lawyer in Jacksonville. I asked her name. "Charlotte something. I'll have to look it up. I think she's a member."

Charlotte? *My* Charlotte?

I went to the bag drop and waited in the cart until a late

model Lexus pulled up to the curb. Dark-tinted windows so I couldn't see inside. My Charlotte didn't have a Lexus. She had a Volvo. A valet opened the door and a woman stepped out. It *was* my Charlotte.

"How do you like my new car, Jake?"

"Looks great. I didn't know you played golf."

"I don't. You'll have to teach me."

I groaned. "Charlotte—it takes years. And I'm not a professional. You should sign up—"

"I don't have years, Jake." She came up and threw her arms around me. "I want to get pregnant."

I hardly had time to register shock when she planted a big kiss on my mouth.

"What are you talking about?"

"I'm serious. I'll be forty soon. And I want to have children."

This seemed to be the 'new' Charlotte. She had never kissed me like that. The valet and a couple of bag drop guys stood by watching us with big grins on their faces.

"Charlotte—I don't want to get married."

"Me, neither. But you can be the father of my children. You won't have to do anything. I'll raise them and support them and put them through college."

"So I'll just be the sperm donor? Like a stud horse?"

She laughed. "More than that. I forgot to tell you, Jake. I love you."

I stared at her goggle-eyed while the bag drop guys clapped and whistled. "I suppose we could get married down the road. Eventually. Maybe."

"There's plenty of time to talk about that. In the meantime, you need to teach me a few things."

"Like golf and—"

"I promise I'll be an eager student."

"Gavronski–8:42," someone said over the the PA system.

Charlotte and I played eighteen holes. She dumped six balls in the water, hit two golf carts, and lost one ball in a tree. In the process I discovered two things: one, she *was* an eager student and she learned fast; two, she has some tits. I hadn't really noticed this before because I hadn't ever gotten that close to her. Now I was standing behind her every couple of holes, trying to show her how to grip the club and swing through the ball. This got me more acquainted with the contours of her body.

Charlotte and I did eventually get married. When the kids were four and six we decided that they could be denied certain benefits down the road, not to mention that they were being teased at the Christian school they attended for having a mommy and daddy 'living in sin.' In fact, we were living together by that time in a spacious condo on the St. Johns River. But I objected to the kids being in a school that condemned cohabitation, abortion, homosexuality and female priests. It was this last prohibition that convinced Charlotte that it was time to transfer the kids to a secular–and much better–school.

As for marriage itself, I'm okay with it. And so is Charlotte. Once a year, we get together with Elena and her brood, which now includes three grandchildren and two step children nearly as old as she is. She married a software executive twenty years her senior who bought the beach house and paid off the construction loans. Max would never recognize the place. It's a paradigm of good taste and fine art.

All in all, it's a good life. Charlotte still works like a Trojan, twelve-hour days. I'm sort of a househusband, dabbling in real estate and playing golf. I also write short stories. Eventually, if I can squeeze it in between open houses and golf games, I intend to write a novel. Charlotte thinks I ought to write one about our experience in Russia.

And Max? According to Anna Pavlovna, he was released from the Lubyanka after six years and is now running for president of Russia.